Orgasmic Erotica

Erotic Adult XXX Short Stories Featuring Gangbangs, Anal, BDSM, Threesomes, Lesbian, BDSM, First Times, Daddies, Roleplay, Cuckold, Femdom, Domination & Submission, Taboo, and more

Jade St. James

indirect, which are incurred as a result of the use of the information contained within this document, including, but not limited to, — errors, omissions, or inaccuracies.

Contents

Introduction   7

1. Daddy Delivers   9
  by Luisa Martinez

2. The Senator   23
  by J. Parissi

3. The Gang Watches Football   39
  by Anya Keller

4. Chelsea Gets What She Wants   53
  by Felicia de Armas

5. Smack   69
  by Calliope Barnes

6. Going Pro on Your First Time   85
  by Randall Kim-Collins

7. The Pastor's Daughter   101
  by Paulette Marsh

8. Who Is in Charge Tonight?   115
  by John Sharma

9. One, Two, Three   131
  by Genevra Wilson

10. Big Enough for Sheri   147
  by Celeste Watts

Conclusion   159

Introduction

Hello friends,

I'm thrilled to present to you my first collection of erotic fiction!

Hi, my name is Jade St. James, and I'm a writer, an editor, a teacher...a real multi-hyphenate. But my passion is, well, dirty stories.

I've been collecting stories from friends and collaborators to share with you, and I think you're going to love what we've come up with.

I've tried to include a wide variety of themes: from romance to pure filth! And the narrators for the audio version are guaranteed to curl your toes.

I know you'll have a fun and sexy time... either by yourself, in your private moments, or enjoy these stories with your partner!

Have fun!

Your new best friend,
Jade

Daddy Delivers
by Luisa Martinez

My bookstore was as quiet as my sex life. That wasn't something that I was proud of. But I refused to go on dating sites. It wasn't that I was pretentious or anything like that. I just wanted the type of person to want to find love that way. I couldn't be attracted to a man who was on a dating site, to begin with. And again, I know that sounds pretentious, but I wanted a man who had so much going on in his life that he didn't need love. Maybe that was just toxic.

"Where is the romance section? You know, the smut?" a customer asked me while passing the front desk.

"It's over in the left corner right by the bathrooms."

The woman smiled. "Thank you. You should

move it closer to the checkout or where you can find it."

She wasn't wrong. Women loved that stuff. And I knew exactly why they loved that stuff. Because I was one of those women. And I guess I'd bashfully put that section of books in the back because I couldn't admit to myself that I wanted it. It was embarrassing. But I wanted a daddy. I wanted a man who didn't necessarily need me but could take control. And in today's world, to say that as a woman isn't the most popular thing. Women fight for their independence. Women fight for equality every single day, and there I was standing behind a counter wanting a man to be my daddy in the bedroom.

But I was shy. I had my principles. And as I organized the counter, I knew that finding a man like that was difficult. Most men were conditioned to think that romance movies or romance books written by Nicholas Sparks were how we wanted them to act. So you would get the nice guy. You would get the timid guy. And those were the type of dates that I always wound up on. My attraction would tank, my pussy would go dry, and there would not be a second date or a hookup. So what was a girl like me to do? She was to go to that smut section, as the woman called it, and fantasize. Sometimes those fantasies would work, other times they would just be poor excuses for what I couldn't handle in my real life. Oh well. I wasn't about to throw a pity party.

I did what I always do at night: thrust myself into work. This was my technique whenever I thought a little bit too much about my own life. It was never good to dwell. That's what I learned. Especially for someone who was very thirsty and not in the drinking water sense. I had everything that I'd ever wanted. That was the truth. Except for one thing. I had my successful bookstore. But I didn't have love. I didn't have the sexual satisfaction that I desired. Now I sounded like one of those characters in the books that the woman was just talking about.

"Just these," the woman said as she put two books down.

I recognized one because I had read it. "This one, *Her Deep Pride,* is really good. I read this one twice," I told her.

She nodded and looked interested in what I was saying. It's always nice to have someone excited about books, especially the ones that I liked. "That's great to hear because I can never find one that I'm truly enthralled with. I just want one of those books that I'm not going to be able to put down, you know what I mean?"

"Well, this is the book. You have my word."

She laughed a little bit. "You know, there's still a stigma with these books. But I think that's some realism to this stuff. People just don't want to admit to it."

It was so weird hearing her say something that I believed with my entire heart. "Well, if people like that do exist, why don't they come out of the closet and face the world so that these books don't have a stigma?"

The way that I asked that question received a look from her as if we were both in the same world but had no answers. "Maybe they will one day. The closet is not a place that you want to be in. Are we talking about gay people or are we talking about people who like daddies?"

We both laughed at that.

When she left, of course, my mind was fixated on my life—something that I wanted to avoid but couldn't after that conversation. It was like I had become even more hyper-aware of my situation. So my technique of working it off didn't work. I couldn't get out of my head.

On top of that, everything changed. Everything changed when I looked out my window. Usually, I had this skinny older UPS driver who would drop off a lot of the shipments to the store. But on that day, there was this muscular Spanish man with stubble on his face and eyes that couldn't allow me to look away. It wasn't that I had always chosen to be with white men, my race. It just happened that way. I was attracted to any type of man. But suddenly looking at this Spanish UPS driver, I felt like my chances of getting with someone outside of what I'd always known had increased. He had sex eyes.

My heart started to race in anticipation of him walking into the store. It was kind of foolish, but it was also just like all of the characters I would read about. It was the perfect situation to live out my fantasies. Of course, things like that didn't happen in real life. So I had to brace for that.

But I didn't have much time to brace because the man walked in. On his uniform, right on the chest, there was a tag that said *Fuentes*. I could only assume that that was his last name. "How are you doing today? This is my new route so I think I'll be seeing more of you."

He was so direct and assertive in the way that he spoke. There was not an ounce of him that lacked confidence, and I liked that.

"No complaints there. I'm always down to meet a new friend."

He smiled. "I hope I'm not out of place for saying this"—whatever he would say, he was putting down boxes as he spoke—"but you're incredibly beautiful."

My cheeks went hot. I almost had to pinch myself because I had never been spoken to by a man like that before. The men I dealt with were never that direct. "Why, thank you. I appreciate that."

"Just sign here. And you're good to go."

My cheeks were still red, and I was going into panic mode because I didn't want the interaction to end. Even though I knew that I would probably see him the next day or sometime that week, I didn't want this man with his spicy cologne to walk out of my shop. I signed for the package, though. Because that was the natural order of things.

"You have beautiful handwriting," he said. The way that he was speaking to me almost made me feel like he was a paid actor. Because everything that he was saying was everything that I wanted him to say. I thought that I was being pranked or something.

I gained the confidence to look him in the eye and say, "You have a lot of compliments today. I enjoy that."

"I'm glad. But I should probably stop so I don't get fired. In today's world, speaking like that could get one in trouble."

I giggled. I couldn't remember the last time I'd giggled. But I did like I was some sort of high school girl. "You will only get in trouble with me if I find out that you speak like this to every woman that you drop a package off to. But that's probably the case because why would you speak to me out of all the other women in the world like this?"

He didn't break eye contact one bit. Those deep brown eyes of his made me wet with just one look. "Do you find it hard to believe that you're that beautiful? Because that's exactly why I'm talking to you like this. I saw you through the window. I saw your curves. The dark red hair of yours. I've never been with a redhead or a white woman. But my God, I should probably stop."

"What if I told you that I wanted you to keep going? That I liked everything that you were saying?"

Speaking of everything that he was saying, I couldn't believe that the conversation we were having was happening. Things like that didn't happen to me. They happened in the books that were on the shelves of my store. I never thought that I would be in the shoes of one of those characters. But there he was, standing before me on the other side of that counter, smelling delicious, looking delicious, and everything in between.

"Well then, I guess I'm not going to stop talking."

* * *

It was all a blur how I got to his place. I mean of course, if I tried to think about how it all went down, I would be able to recall it. I didn't have amnesia or anything like that. But I was in his home. We were kissing. That's all we had started to do. Our lips were wild. It was like we were two virgins. His lips were a little bit aggressive, far more aggressive than mine. But I liked every little movement that he made. Every little flick of the tongue made me wetter by the second. I was living out this dream, a fantasy; everything that I ever wanted would just be his kiss. I wanted more. It was crazy to think that we were kissing and I just wanted more and more. You would think that I would be somewhat satisfied with just lips. But no, he drove me crazy.

The next thing that he did was run his hands through my hair. He gave it a little pull. I let out a little moan while kissing him. His touch was rough.

He moved me over to the couch where he was gentle enough to lay me down. But once I was down, it all began.

His hand went right to my breast. The squeeze

that he gave it hurt in the best of ways. Could he be that daddy figured I wanted? Absolutely. Was he willing to be that daddy figure? There was maybe an eighty percent chance. Just by the way that he was handling me, making me feel small, making me feel like a little, it was the closest that I was ever going to get. And I had zero complaints about that.

It was time to test the waters.

"Squeeze my titty a little harder, Daddy."

He smiled and gave me those eyes of his. "Oh, you're into that type of stuff, huh? I like that. You want to be my little?" He put one hand around my neck and gave it a little squeeze. It was nothing to hurt me, just enough to turn me on. I couldn't believe it. I couldn't believe that I was living out what I had been dreaming about for a very long time; for as long as I had been reading those books I had always put myself in the shoes of those characters and dreamed about getting manhandled by a man in the best of ways.

"I am into that type of stuff, Daddy. I want you to take me. Do whatever you want with me."

He smiled again, but this time, it was a devious smile. It was the type of smile where I didn't know what I was going to be in for. And I liked that uncertainty, that little bit of danger. You couldn't get that feeling anywhere else in life. The only place I could get it was right before the man who I only knew as Fuentes. It was crazy to think that he knew my full name as Claire Denver, and I only knew his last name. But it was fitting. He was more than just a name. *Yeah, become my daddy.*

He wasted no time and took my top off. My nipples went hard at the thought of him seeing them without the bra. That didn't last long, either. He unhooked it with one hand. I had kind of expected that.

The second that my perky red nipples entered the room, he started to suck on them. He had the other one that was free in his hand giving it a nice squeeze. Every time he did that, I felt myself getting a little bit wetter.

My nipples disappeared between his lips. He flicked them with his tongue. I was like an instrument in his presence. It seemed like he couldn't get enough of me because sucking my titties didn't last that long.

He brought his hands down to my yoga pants and yanked them off. I didn't realize that the underwear had been with them as well. My pussy had entered the room.

For whatever reason, I felt a little bashful having

him see my slit. For one, I would be soaked. And it was something embarrassing about getting so turned on. The second thing was the fact that he was just so manly. He had this caveman aura about him. It was like being objectified in the best of ways. The vibe that I was feeling I would never forget. It was just one of those experiences that changed a person.

He started to eat me out. His tongue was like magic. The tricks and turns that he was doing with it, I couldn't even imagine what he would do down there with it. It just felt amazing. I watched his forehead move about as if it was feasting. Again, objectified in the best of ways. I felt like his dinner. And he was enjoying every bit of me. The way that he soaked me up with his tongue, I had never been with a man like that before. I had never been with a man who enjoyed it so much. As terrible as it may sound, it always felt like a job when I looked at them. But this man, Fuentes, made me feel special. He made me feel like I was the only woman in the world. And that kind of felt like I owed him a debt of gratitude.

So when he was finished having his way with me, I pushed him onto the bed and started to unbuckle his pants. But he wasn't having it. He wanted to stay in control without even needing to say that. Because he pushed me back down and started to undo his pants as well. He stayed near my head, which meant I knew what he was going to do. It was what I wanted to do with him. But he was going to take charge. He was going to be my daddy. Or better yet, he was my daddy already.

I watched him unbuckle his pants in anticipation of seeing his cock. My heart was racing as I imagined what the thing looked like. I could tell just by the bulge that it was large. The thing was pitching a tent; I just couldn't tell how big it was. The moment was coming, though. Because down came the zipper, and his fingertips clutched the elastic of the boxers. Seconds later, he yanked them down, and I was staring right at this massive cock. It was long, thick, and veiny. I was enthralled with the thing. To say that I got wetter would have been redundant, but it was the truth. I just wanted him to touch my pussy. I had never wanted something so badly. But I had a duty to fulfill. I needed to please him.

The cock came my way, and I took a firm grip. The next thing I knew, I was trying my best to fit the thick thing in my mouth. It was tough to fit in, but I was getting it down. Once it was in there, I began to suck. It wasn't easy pulling the thing in and out, but the more I did, the more I enjoyed it. I could see the ridges and veins going in and out.

At one point, he had to pull out because he was going to come. This meant that it was finally time to get fucked.

"I want you, Daddy. I want you inside of me badly."

His facial expression never changed from that determined look of his. When he was stuffing it in, I felt like my pussy was going to rip. But I liked it at the same time. What followed was Fuentes ramming himself in and out of me. He did that in the missionary position. His face was a mask of passion. It was like he was putting all his effort into it while enjoying himself.

He had one hand on my breast while he did it. The sex lasted what felt like a good, long time. And when it was over, he yanked his shit out and squirted all over my stomach.

We lay there next to one another after the deed was done.

"Aren't you glad that I dropped the package off?" Fuentes asked.

I started to laugh. "I'm very glad that you're my new delivery man. You can deliver that dick whenever you want."

We both laughed.

I didn't know what was going to come of me and

Fuentes. But no matter what happened, I had lived out a bit of my dream, that storybook dirty romance that I had always craved. And if it was going to last, then I most certainly knew that I would get my happy ending.

Because he was a new daddy.

The Senator
by J. Parissi

"I DON'T THINK we're going to be able to push this bill any further." He sat back in his chair and tapped his pen against the desk. In the background, he heard the steady rise and fall of conversation outside his door, punctuated by the occasional ringing of the phone.

Philip McManus sat up straighter in his chair and frowned. "I already told you that I'd do my best, Senator Hodgins. I've taken this bill as far as it's going to go."

With a sigh, he pressed two fingers to his temples and rubbed in slow, circular motions. "I'll put it up for a vote, yes."

A short while later, he hung up the call and set his phone down with a grimace. Slowly, he stood up, peeled off his jacket, and draped it over the back of his chair. Then he stood in front of the large window, overlooking the glittering city skyline. Far below, he saw cars rushing past in either direction while people walked brusquely in their business suits, phones pressed to their ears.

When his assistant, Martha, knocked on the door and poked her head in, he was sitting at his desk, leafing through the stack of paperwork there. "Yes, what is it?"

"I'm confirming your lunch order, sir."

He nodded without looking up at her. "Yes, I'll have the usual, thank you."

Martha cleared her throat. "Senator Parish's office called again. She's waiting to hear back about the meeting."

With a frown, he glanced up at her and linked his fingers together. "She doesn't quit, does she?"

Martha blinked, her dark eyes filled with confusion. "Sir?"

"Sent her a gift basket with my apologies and tell her I'll be in touch as soon as possible," Philip replied with a shake of his head. "Damn Democrats. They're like a dog with a bone."

"Yes, sir."

"Hold my calls for the rest of the day unless it's an emergency."

"Your mother called, Senator. She asked me to remind you of tomorrow night's dinner."

He waved her comment away and reached for the glass of water on his desk. "Yes, yes. That's fine. Thank you, Martha."

As soon as she shut the door behind her, he released a deep breath and tugged on his tie. He let it hang askew around his neck and pulled open the first drawer of his desk. After some rummaging around, he found the small burner phone and held it up to his ear. Once he was done with the phone call, he smiled and return his attention to the paperwork on his desk.

Over the next few hours, he poured over every paper until a headache formed in the back of his skull. As the Republican senator for the state of Louisiana, it always felt like his job was never done. Each day when he woke up, he had a litany of decisions that needed to be made and a swarm of people hanging on his every word.

Thankfully, every Friday night, at the end of his work day, he made his way to an apartment in the suburbs, where his mistress, Serena Osbourne, waited for him.

And this Friday was no exception.

Once the sun dipped below the horizon, bathing the world in hues of pink and purple, he stood up and shrugged into his jacket. He hummed underneath his breath as he powered off the laptop, tucked it into the bag, and swung it over his shoulders. On the way out, he nodded in Martha's general direction, and she scrambled to her feet, twin pools of color staining her cheeks.

She waited until he got on the elevator before she relaxed.

Outside, a black car waited for him by the curb. He got into the back seat and looked out the window, at the blur of shapes and colors hurrying past in either direction. A short while later, when they pulled up outside his apartment building, he hurried upstairs and changed out of his clothes. Then he came back down in a pair of jeans, a sweater, and a hat pulled low over his head.

The driver dropped him a block away from the apartment, situated in the middle of the suburbs, with two-story houses on either side, manicured lawns, and driveways with two cars. Paul smiled to himself as he approached the front door of the last house on the block and went around the back.

Serena answered the door dressed in skimpy red

lingerie with a cigarette dangling from her mouth. Her blood red lips lifted into a smile as she pulled him in and gave him a smack on the lips. Once the door clicked shut behind him, she put out the cigarette and led him to his favorite brown leather armchair.

A glass of whiskey was already set out for him. "You always know what to do to make me feel better after a long day."

"Drink," Serena replied with a smile. "I've got a fun night planned for us."

Immediately, he sat down and lifted the glass up to his lips. He eyed her over the rim as she finished setting up the candles, heels clicking against the hardwood floors. As soon as she was done, she wandered over to him and let her robe fall to the floor.

Her smooth, tanned skin glistened underneath the soft glow of the candles.

His fingers twitched at his sides.

Serena tossed her red hair over her shoulders and placed one leg on either side of his lap. "Put your hands on me."

Philip finished his drink in one gulp and placed both hands on her waist. "Like this?"

Serena draped herself over him and moaned. "Grip my waist harder, Senator."

Philip's blood roared in his ears. He dug his nails into her waist, and she bucked against him, breasts straining against the fabric of her bra. When he shifted against her, she drew back and wagged a finger at him.

"That's not how this works, Senator. In this house, I make the rules, remember?"

Philip swallowed. "I know."

"Good. Now put your wrists together." Serena slid off, her hips swaying as she moved away from him. He watched her every movement, desire pooling in the center of his stomach. She opened a drawer in the kitchen, crouched, and rummaged around. Then she returned with a pair of silver handcuffs and a wicked grin.

His cock tightened.

Wordlessly, she climbed back onto him and placed the cool metal around his wrists. "You're all mine, remember?"

"Yes."

Serena gave the restraints a firm tug, and her hand fell between them, rubbing him over his pants. "Yes what?"

Philip bit back a groan. "Yes, mistress."

Serena rubbed him harder. "Good. If you're a good boy, I'm going to reward you, remember? But if you're a bad boy, I'm going to punish you."

Philip licked his lips and nodded.

Serena pulled him to his feet and motioned to the floor. He lay down on the carpet, fully clothed, and waited. After a brief pause, Serena's heels dug into his back, sending waves of delight racing up his spine. He lifted his arms up over his head and groaned. Then Serena was pulling him back up to his feet and tugging him in the direction of the bedroom.

There, she pushed him onto the bed and straddled him.

A moment later, she uncuffed him and placed both hands on her breasts. "Touch me, Philip. I want you to touch me everywhere. I want you to leave me wanting more."

Philip's stomach clenched as he unhooked her bra, allowing her breasts to spill forward. He took one nipple between his teeth and tugged hard. Serena wrapped her legs around his waist and moaned. He moved to the other nipple and sucked and bit until they were both as hard as pebbles. Abruptly, Serena stood up and drew him to his feet.

She used one finger to remove her panties, her eyes never leaving his face.

As soon as she was done, she placed both hands on her hips and arched a brow at him. "Strip."

In one quick move, Philip was out of his shirt and pants, leaving them in a heap on the floor. Once he straightened his back, Serena strode toward him, a determined gleam in her eyes. She pushed him back onto the mattress, climbed on top of him, and kissed him.

She tasted like wine and tobacco, a heady combination that never failed to make his blood boil. All week, he thought of her, and their wild nights together, and what she was going to make him do next. Having discovered her a few months ago, Philip now had no idea how he had ever managed without her.

Serena was exactly what he needed after a long day at the office.

As if she sensed his train of thought, she deepened the kiss and let her hand fall between them so she was stroking him. He bucked against her, but Serena's movements wouldn't change. Instead, she continued to stroke him slowly, each movement more torturous than the last. Eventually, she sat back on her legs and looked directly at him.

"I want you to touch yourself," Serena instructed in a thick voice. "And you're going to watch me while I do the same."

Philip sat up, and by the soft light of the moon, he saw Serena stretch her legs out on either side of her and stroke herself. Two fingers darted in between her wet mounds, covered in a thick patch of hair. She used her other hand to push her breasts together and moaned.

He ran his hands up and down his shift, heart hammering wildly against his chest.

Fuck.

Philip wasn't sure how long he was going to last if he kept watching her, craving her as she did those things to herself. Serena's hazel eyes flew open, and she gave him a coy smile. She quickened her pace and bucked. Moments later, she writhed and spasmed, riding out her orgasm as she did. His grip on his member tightened as his hips rose up off the mattress.

With a smirk, Serena crawled forward and pressed two fingers to his lips. "Taste me, Philip."

His mouth parted, and he licked her juices off her fingers, the salty taste riling him up even more. Serena placed a hand on top of his and shook her head. "Not yet. I don't want you coming too soon."

Philip sat up, cupped her face in his hand, and kissed her. "I want to have some fun too."

Serena chuckled and shifted so her back was pressed against the headboard. "You will, but I'm going to decide when."

And he loved that about their time together.

Here he was free to have her order him around without worrying about the consequences.

She brought her head to a rest against the pillow, spread her legs apart and smiled at him. "I want your tongue between my legs, Philip."

Philip gave her a slow, sensual grin. "I thought you'd never ask."

Quickly, he lowered himself onto the mattress, pressing hot, open-mouthed kisses along the inside of her thighs. Then he sat back on his legs, positioned his mouth at her clit, and pressed a soft kiss there. Serena whimpered and lifted her hips up off the mattress.

"Don't stop," Serena breathed, her eyes squeezing shut. "Don't stop, please."

All of the blood rushed to Philip's groin as he used two fingers to part her wet folds. With one last look at her face, he buried his face in her pussy and licked. Serena's fingers wove themselves through his hair and tugged. She bucked and writhed against him while he explored every inch of her, sucking and licking as he did.

She tasted better and better every time.

He wanted to stay between her legs forever.

When she shifted, drawing him closer, Philip glanced up and saw her studying him through hooded eyes. "Fuck me harder with your tongue, Philip. I want to scream your name."

Philip placed one hand on her breasts, and the other dug into her waist. He used his legs to pin her in place as he drove her closer and closer to the brink of ecstasy. She writhed and thrashed underneath him, muttering incomprehensibly underneath her breath. As soon as her grip on the back of his neck tightened, he quickened his pace.

Serena cried out his name as she came.

He crawled up to kiss her, letting her taste her juices on his lips. Serena smiled into his mouth and sat up straighter. She maneuvered them so he was flat on his back and she was on top again. Before his hands could move to her waist, she grabbed both of his wrists and secured them with the rope dangling from her bed.

"You're at my mercy, Senator," Serene teased with a wicked smile. "I can do whatever I want to you."

Philip tugged on the restraints and swallowed past the dryness in his throat. "What are you going to do to me?"

"Whatever I want," Serena whispered, pausing to pepper his neck with kisses. She kissed her way down to his chest and stopped when she reached the smattering of hair leading down to his engorged member. Looking up at him, she wrapped her mouth around the top and sucked.

A jolt of electricity exploded within him.

Holy shit.

His hips rose up off the mattress as she took more and more of him inside of her. Her eyes stayed on his face, wide and full of hunger as she continued to pleasure him. He tugged on his restraints, itching to wind his fingers through her hair and around the back of her neck.

Serena placed her hands on either side of the mattress and took all of him into her mouth. His eyes rolled to the back of his head, and his ears began to ring. He bucked against her, and she dug her nails into his waist. Wave after wave of desire built within him until he hurtled towards the edge.

Abruptly, Serena stopped and used the back of her hand to wipe her mouth.

Then she threw one leg on either side of him so

she was straddling him. She ran her hands down the front of her chest, pausing to press her breasts together. With a smile, she adjusted herself and sank onto him. Philip's eyes flew open as she ground against him, eliciting a growl.

"Look at how hard you are," Serena purred, her voice dropping an octave. "You've been waiting to fuck me, haven't you?"

Philip fixed his gaze on hers and cleared his throat. "Yes, mistress."

"When you're at your desk, making all those decisions, all you want is for me to be there, don't you?"

Philip groaned.

Serena slowed and dug her nails into his waist. "I can't hear you."

Philip swallowed. "Yes, I think about you all the time."

Serena lowered her head and pressed her mouth to his neck. She licked and sucked on the sensitive skin there while she bounced up and down, her breasts pressed between them.

"You've thought about fucking me on your desk, haven't you?"

Philip growled into her neck. "I have."

Serena sat up and panted. In one quick move,

she undid his restraints so that his hands fell to her waist. "Show me, Philip. Show me how you want to fuck me."

Philip eased out of her and flipped her onto her back. She rose up so she was on all fours, her ass in the air. He placed one hand on either side of her waist and positioned himself behind her. In one quick move, he was inside of her, stretching her to the hilt and groaning.

She felt so damn good.

Too damn good.

He began to rock back and forth against her while she panted and moaned, the sounds reverberating inside of his head. His hands darted underneath and flicked her nipples, moving back and forth between the two until they were hard as pebbles. In the glass of the closet across the room, he saw the two of them as he slammed in and out of her.

His pulse quickened.

He needed this.

He needed her.

Serena bucked against him and held herself up on her elbows. "That's it, Philip. Fuck me. Fuck me harder."

He brought his head to a rest against her flushed back, glistening with sweat, and cursed. The bed dipped and creaked underneath their weight. In the distance, he heard dogs howling and the screeching of tires against the asphalt. Serena twisted an arm over her head and gripped the back of his neck.

When she squeezed, he nipped on the inside of her wrist. "You feel so good, Serena. Fuck."

"That's it," Serena encouraged, in a breathy voice. "Keep fucking me, Senator."

Philip squeezed his eyes shut, pinned her arms over her back, and thrust.

When Serena's body began to writhe and spasm, and her breath quickened, he eased out and slammed back into her. Over and over, he thrust in and out until his breathing changed, and his movements turned frantic and wild.

Serena squeezed her legs together and rode out her orgasm.

His own release followed quickly after as his entire body jerked, and he emptied himself into her. As soon as he was done, he rolled off of her and collapsed onto the next. Next to him, he heard Serena sit up and rummage around in the bedside drawer. A heartbeat later, her face was lit up with the flame of a lighter.

"I wonder what your constituents would think of this." A thick ring of smoke surrounded her face as she smiled at him. "Conservative Senator Philip McManus likes to be dominated by women."

"They're never going to find out," Philip told her with a smile. He stood up, reached for his pants, and pulled out his wallet. "I pay you well to keep it a secret, remember?"

Once he set the usual five hundred dollars down on the nightstand, Serena's lips lifted into a smile. "Always a pleasure, Senator."

"I'll see you next week."

The Gang Watches Football
by Anya Keller

SOMETHING WASN'T EXACTLY right with Roy. Now and then, he would close up. And Samantha couldn't ignore it. It just seemed like he had something on his mind like he was preoccupied.

This behavior was a little bit extra one night while she was making him dinner. She had been serving him, and the only thing that was normal about him was his eyes. He was giving her the "sex eyes." After all, he loved her ginger hair and curves, and no matter what mood he would be in, that would always be the same. But it was his silence that drove her crazy. He was polite. He made a little conversation, but it just always seemed like he was thinking about something else.

They had a relationship where they were very

open with one another. So for him to not be communicative was strange, almost alarming. And as much as they were able to communicate with one another regularly, Samantha found it difficult to bring up the fact that he was acting the way that he was. Because she didn't want to start problems. She didn't want to seem like she was nitpicking. So she placed the meatloaf down in the center of the table and cut into it. She gave Roy a little smile when she did so.

He smiled back, but it was a little forced. Again she couldn't tell whether or not she was making things up in her mind. And that drove her crazy. But after serving Roy and then herself, she sat down and did her best to ignore it once more. Normalcy was all she was after. But Roy was the furthest thing from being normal.

"So, how was your day?" she asked him.

His eyes never left his plate. She tried to convince herself that it was because of her good cooking. "It was good. Mitch from Marketing got fired today, so we were all kind of happy. That guy was a douche."

Samantha smiled. "Yeah, I remember you telling me that you disliked him. Those pompous people never last."

Three seconds of silence filled the air before Roy said, "Yep."

One word had never driven her so crazy before. What was going on? Why was he so elusive? Why couldn't he just tell her what was on his mind? It had to be bad if he was hiding it. Her mind ran in a million different directions trying to figure out what it could be. If there was ever a time for her to be psychic, that was it. She just wished and craved that she could take a peek inside his mind and figure out what was going on in there. Did it have something to do with her at all? Was he going through something?

She did her best to eat dinner and ignore everything. She told herself that she wasn't going to be the type of person to pry. But as the forks clanged against the plate and silence filled the room, she needed to ask him. There was no way around it.

"Roy, I need to know what's been bothering you. You're not the same. You've been quiet with me all week. Maybe even all month. And I've bit my tongue and tried to tell myself that nothing is wrong, but I can't do this anymore. I'm really upset. I want to know what's on your mind. I want to know what you're hiding."

When Roy finally looked up from his plate, he wore a mask of shock. Samantha couldn't blame him for that. This had come out of left field, after all. And it wasn't like her to put him on the spot. She was usually very understanding. But at that moment, there wasn't much to understand. Everything was so vague. Everything felt so mysterious. It was making her heart race at an alarming rate.

Maybe Roy could see how worked up she had been because there was a bit of understanding in his eyes. He didn't look like he was caught off guard. It almost looked like the game was up, and he could finally reveal whatever it was that was on his mind. That scared her, though, in a way. As much as she wanted to know what was going on, she was also afraid of what it could be.

Was he deathly ill?

Had he cheated on her?

Was he secretly gay or something?

Nothing was off limits in terms of her imagination. She would think the worst but hope for anything else.

"I don't want you to be upset with me if I say it to you. I also don't want you to think of me as weird," Roy said to her.

That didn't calm her down one bit. It only made things seem worse. But at that moment, she was able to wrangle her thoughts a bit and just listen. She knew what she had to say to get him to talk. "Whatever it is, I'm not going to be mad. I just want to know what it is so we can clear the air here."

He let out a sigh and put down his fork. "I have fantasies, Samantha. One specific fantasy. I know we've been dating for three years. It feels like everything's been out in the open. But to be honest, I've been hiding this fantasy for about six months. It all started when you wore that maid outfit on Halloween."

She remembered the sexy maid outfit vividly. It was one of the most provocative outfits she had ever worn. It was a costume, and they had attended a party as she wore it. She never had intended for it to be on his mind six months later. And in what way? She had so many questions and knew that whatever she thought of in her head would probably not align with what he was about to say. "I'm going to need you to be more specific, Roy. Okay, you liked my costume. What does that have to do with you being quiet and silent and all this? You have to understand, it's driving me crazy."

"All right, look, I'll cut to the chase. I want to have a gangbang. I want all my friends to fuck you while you serve during the Super Bowl."

It was not even close to the images that she'd had

in her head. It almost didn't feel real hearing those words come from his mouth. Where did such a fantasy come from? Why did he want something like that? Those were questions that she had, and they were questions that should have been asked to him directly.

"I have a lot of questions, Roy."

"I knew that you would. And I hope I didn't ruin your appetite or whatever. I'm sorry that I have these things. They're just—"

"Why would you want your friends to have sex with me?"

It was funny, and it wasn't funny, because she had thought about such a thing before. She had imagined having sex with some of his friends. But she considered that normal. Everyone had fleeting thoughts. Everyone had little fantasies that they had to push to the back of their mind. But it was kind of funny that he was bringing it up and to the forefront.

"I don't know why I have this fantasy, Samantha. Believe me, sometimes I feel terrible for it and sometimes I feel like I'm betraying you. But at the same time, you can't deny what you want. And that's what I want. I just want to see it once. I just want to watch my friends have sex with you in that little maid outfit. I guess part of me just wants to face that part of myself. If that makes sense. You know it's an inse-cure thing to imagine someone else having sex with you. Let alone best friends. So to do that, face it, and pull that Band-Aid off, that turns me on."

Samantha's heart was still racing. But for different reasons. She had an okay to have sex with three other men: his best friends, Jacob, Patrick, and Fabian. She went from thinking about only having sex with him for the rest of her life to suddenly having three other dicks inside of her. That just didn't feel real. It felt wrong and right at the same time.

"Well, I don't know how I feel about this right now, Roy. Having sex with your friends is a big implication. It would change the entire relationship."

"Would it, though?"

Samantha wondered if she had time to think about her answer. It felt as though it required one right away. "I don't know, Roy. There's a reason that not many couples do that. I don't want to ruin us. I don't want you to see me differently if I were to do that."

"So it's on the table."

Her lips pursed. "Maybe. But only if like, you were a hundred percent on board with it, and I knew that nothing between you and me would change."

"Nothing will. I promise. I'm the one that brought this up. I don't ask this next question for anything other than pure curiosity. Why do you think you'd be on board with it?"

Samantha had to dig deep for that question. It felt like it should have been right on the tip of her tongue. But it wasn't. "That's a hard question to answer. I don't know. I guess because it's so taboo. Because I trust our relationship, it turns me on to know that you would allow me to have sex with someone else. Not that I want to have sex with someone else, but I don't know."

Roy smiled, and she knew that her answer had been the right one. If there even was such a thing in this type of conversation. "You have absolutely nothing to worry about. This is what I want. And as long as you're comfortable with it, we can do it without any issues. Do I have a yes?"

Samantha looked down at her plate, and suddenly her appetite had returned. When she looked back at Roy, she said, "It is a yes. But again, I will not tolerate any problems after this all happens."

"You have my word, baby."

It has been two weeks since they'd had that discussion. Those two weeks have flown by. The day has finally come. Jacob, Patrick, and Fabian all arrived at the house on Super Bowl Sunday. It wasn't that she wasn't looking forward to it. She just had nervous energy. Now and then her hands would shake at the prospect of getting banged by four men, including her husband.

She heard the doorbell from the bedroom. She was standing before their full-length mirror in the maid outfit. Her cleavage was on full display. The skirt was only a few inches from her needs. It left both little and a lot to the imagination. It may have been a weird thing to wear, but the bright side of it all would say she felt tremendously sexy in that outfit. She was a very conservative Ginger. So wearing something like that made her feel like a superhero especially knowing that Roy loved it so much. She could have believed that three other men were going to take it off of her at some point. But she looked herself in the eyes and in that mirror, I gave a deep breath. It was time to help row and live out his fantasy.

When she walked downstairs, she could hear football playing on the TV, and boys talking amongst themselves, and this caused her heart rate to increase.

Walking off the steps, everyone stopped for a moment, acknowledged her, and then went about their business. The role-playing had begun. She was no longer Samantha Albright. She was the maid. The sexy maid.

So the sexy maid had to play the part. That made her figure that she should say, "Do you guys need anything?"

It was Roy who looked up first. He smiled as though she was doing a good job with her role-playing which made her feel good. They gave her goosebumps. She couldn't wait to get started. It amazed her how into it she could be given the fact that she considered herself a prude half the time. "I'll have a beer," Roy said to her.

It was crazy how his little demand could get her all riled up. He was her boyfriend. She had known him for three years and yet pretending to be his maid and getting him a beer, it felt like a whole different world.

She went to the kitchen and did as he had asked. She got him a nice cold beer. When she handed it to him, he held on to her hand. "Light Patrick a cigar."

She held back her smile and did as he told her to

do. Patrick gave her a deep eye contact issue with his cigar. The thing was in his mouth while she did it.

"What do you think about this rack, Patrick? She's got a nice big rack, right?" Roy asked him. For the briefest of seconds, Patrick looked as though he didn't know how to answer. But then it's like he snapped into character. Because he said, "Yeah, she's got a great fuckin' rack. I think I want to see those titties."

"I can share my maid. Let's take a look at her titties, shall we?" Roy said.

They all gathered around her and her goose-bumps arrived. She couldn't believe what was about to happen. There was no stopping it, though.

Roy started to unbutton the front of her maid's outfit. The eyes of Patrick, Jacob, and Fabian all remained on her chest. Jacob wanted someone that had reddish hair like hers. Patrick had auburn hair. And Fabian had black hair. Fabian had a lot of stereotypical Italian things about him, like the way that he wore his gold chains to the white tank top. He was a guinea.

She had always looked at them as just her boyfriend's friends. Suddenly she could look at them in a sexual light. She wondered if Patrick had a big cock. She wondered what Fabian was like as a kisser.

She wondered whether or not Jacob was aggressive when he was sexual. They were all questions that she usually had to force out of her mind, but not today. Today everything was different.

When the top of her maid outfit was off, she stood before them in a bra. Fabian walked her over to the couch, unhooked the back of her bra, and laid her down. "I think we should do something with this woman. Should we take her bra off to see what these titties look like?"

The guys nodded.

Patrick took her bra off. She glanced down to look at her nipples. She couldn't believe how hard they were. She also couldn't believe that Fabian took one between his fingers and started to squeeze a little bit, while Jacob sucked on the other. Roy laughed at that.

"Have your way with her, fellas," I said.

Samantha's heart started to race. It felt so good to have one man grabbing her titty while another one sucked on it.

Patrick started to pull down her skirt while Fabian watched. They were like animals.

Roy was in the back taking his pants off. The other guys only glanced over to see what he was doing, and then they looked away. She found it tremendously sexy that there was going to be four dicks in the room despite them all being friends. It was so taboo. It was everything that she wasn't used to.

Fabian started to take his pants off as well. She kept her eyes trained on him because she wanted to see what his dick looked like. When it was out, It was smaller than Roy's. For whatever reason, she found it funny. She took pride in the size of Roy's penis.

But while she had been doing that, she hadn't realized that Patrick was in the middle of taking her panties off. In the room, her pussy was finally out. There was a bit of a ginger bush covering her lips. But that didn't stop Patrick from eating her out. Fabian went back to sucking on her nipples while he did that.

The first dick that went into her was Jacob's. Roy was jerking off while that happened. He started as missionary but turned her over and went into doggy.

At one point, he pulled out, and seconds later, the dick felt different. When she looked behind herself, it was Patrick. In and out he thrust as Roy watched. There didn't seem to be one ounce of insecurity in Roy, and that turned Samantha on. The only thing that she felt bad about was possibly coming via one of his friends. That felt wrong. But the more that they traded off, the closer she felt to climaxing. There was nothing that she could do to slow that down.

She looked at Roy with a face filled with pleasure. "You're allowed to come, baby," he said to her.

That was the green light for her. With Fabian's cock inside of her, she released, clutching the couch as hard as she could while her whole body experienced orgasm.

The deed had been done. She had been part of a gangbang for Roy. And it didn't seem like it would hurt their relationship at all.

Maybe it would make it even better. Only time would tell how it would affect the relationship in the long term. But she liked how he'd handled things. She had a good feeling that everything would be fine. It made her see him in a different light altogether.

Chelsea Gets What She Wants
by Felicia de Armas

THE SUMMER after freshman year of college had never tasted so good for Chelsea. Or maybe it was just the spiked seltzers. Either way, she was having the time of her life at the beach house belonging to Henry. There were also several friends that she went to college with. They were all celebrating a good time, but Chelsea had one thing on her mind. And that thing was a person named Jordan.

He was in the back playing beer pong with Michael while the sun went down. She wanted to be out there with him. She also wanted to finally muster up the courage to tell him how she felt.

She wanted to fuck him. She had desired that since the beginning of college. They had chemistry together. And they had both taken it as an elective by accident. That was one of the few conversations that she'd had with him that seemed to be a sheer coincidence that could lead to something more. Or at least that was the hopeful romantic in her. She couldn't tell. The seltzer was getting to her brain.

She was sitting on the couch watching *Jersey Shore* reruns with Ashley. They had been talking about all sorts of things. But they were trivial compared to the thoughts that she was having about Jordan. He was tall, with dark hair, tattoos, green eyes, and muscles—everything that she wanted to have in her hands. He was everything that she wanted in her bed as well.

"You don't seem like you're having fun. You seem preoccupied," Ashley said while Heather mixed more drinks in the kitchen.

"I'm good," Chelsea said. She couldn't think of anything else to say. She was a very bad liar. But Ashley, her friend of many years, knew that.

"You keep looking at Jordan. Do you want to go shoot your shot? You didn't come here for no reason, you know."

Chelsea shrugged. "I don't necessarily feel like getting rejected by him today. Call me crazy. I'd rather enjoy myself."

Ashley laughed, and so did Heather. "What

makes you think he's going to reject you? You have great boobs. You have an awesome figure. Yeah, great personality. You're funny," Heather said. There is absolutely no reason for you to feel insecure. You should walk over there with confidence."

Chelsea's face went red. "You think so? He doesn't pay much mind to me. It's one thing to have confidence and it's another thing to have Jordan's confidence. I don't know if I can meet him on his level, you know?"

"I say you just go up to him," Ashley said.

Chelsea shrugged and continued to drink her seltzer. "Maybe later."

After that conversation, they continue to watch TV. And sure, Chelsea continued to think about Jordan and sneak glances at him through the glass back door.

She hadn't been lying about his confidence. He was just one tall glass of ego. And all she could think about was riding him. It kind of shocked her how horny she was. She wasn't usually like that and couldn't tell if it was the alcohol or not.

After an hour or so, they all went outside to start barbecuing. The summer air tickled Chelsea in all the right places.

"You know what you could do." Ashley startled

Chelsea from behind. "Sorry, I didn't mean to scare you." She pulled Chelsea aside. "Don't look at me like I'm crazy, but I did hear a rumor that Jordan is into anal."

Chelsea's mouth almost fell to the floor. It wasn't like her and Ashley to talk sex. Especially not in that depth. They always had unspoken boundaries. There were just some things they didn't cover. "Ashley, I appreciate the info, but I think you're a little drunk."

Ashley laughed in a drunk type of way. "Maybe a little bit. But that doesn't change the fact that my info is true. He likes it a lot. I heard his ex talking about it once. She was the only girl that ever let him do it. If you want to get his attention, go for the butt."

Chelsea's cheeks were like the tomatoes sitting next to the grill. "Again, Ashley"—she patted her back—"thanks for the info."

Chelsea went over to Heather, who had offered to play a game of beer pong. Jordan was by the grill cooking by himself. While she played beer pong, she did keep stealing glances again at Jordan.

"You can't keep doing this, Chelsea. Go over to him. Just do it. You want me to be a wingman?"

Chelsea hated how obvious she was being. In addition to not talking about sex with her friends, she also didn't like to talk about her deep desires like that. But because of the alcohol, it was impossible to hide it. "Whatever."

She finally took the advice of her friends and walked over to Jordan. Her heart started to race as she approached him. She had spoken to him some, but not enough to feel comfortable with him. It made her nerves rattle. But it also gave her a surge of energy to combat those nerves. She didn't even know what she was going to say for the icebreaker. She certainly wasn't going to bring up anal. It all had to be natural.

"Hey, you need help cooking?"

He didn't even look at her. He was too busy flipping the burgers. His intensity in doing that even turned her on. "No, I'm good. Thanks, though."

Dejected. That wasn't a strong enough word to describe what she felt at that moment. But her feet remained glued in the position that they were at. "You sure? Those burgers don't look like they're getting cooked right." She completely lied and made that up on the spot. She had no idea where it came from.

After that, Jordan finally looked at her. It sent chills down her spine. The look that he gave her was like lion eyes. She couldn't tell whether it was anger or something else. "You have a lot to say, huh? These burgers are going to kick ass. Unlike you at beer pong."

Even though it was meant as an insult, she liked the little bit of verbal sparring that they had going on. But of course, her tongue got the best of her, and she slipped out in saying, "I'm better at doing anal."

This time, there was a mix of emotions in his eyes. It almost made Chelsea want to break out in laughter. She had finally caught him off guard and broken him a little bit. It gave her a bit of confidence that she needed. "Excuse me?"

"You heard me. So it must be right about you and anal, huh? That's what you like?"

He dropped his spatula. His stunned silence made Chelsea feel like she had the upper hand. "How do you know that?"

She shrugged. "After dinner, I'll let you do it."

He still had a stunned expression on his face. She couldn't hold her laughter in. "You're joking."

"I'm only laughing because you're so shocked. I'm not joking in the slightest." She brought her voice down to a whisper and couldn't believe what she was about to say next. But it was coming out no matter what. "I want you to fuck me. And you can do it in my ass. No lie, no joke. Come get me after dinner."

She walked away with a smile on her face. This was a level of confidence she had never experienced before.

She refused to look back at Jordan because she didn't want to break the illusion. She wanted him to see her as completely confident and committed to what she had just said. She wanted him to feel as though it could happen. But there was just one problem.

She had never done anal before.

Chelsea would have to do more than just say that she would do anal when it came to Jordan. She was going to have to do it. And that was something that she hadn't realized until after she'd said it. Doing anal was something that scared her. She wouldn't even allow her man to go near her butt, let alone put a dick in it. In a way, she hoped that he didn't want to do it. But on the other end of the spectrum, of course, she wanted him to be on board. It was a strange duality that made her nervous. But in a good way. She couldn't complain about her situation whatsoever. It was a win-win in many ways. If he denied her, he at least knew that she wanted him. If things were to progress, then she would have what she always wanted for years.

"What did you say to him?" Ashley asked her.

For a moment, Chelsea didn't know whether or not she wanted to reveal what she had said. She felt downright dirty just thinking about it. "I did what you told me to do. Or whatever both of you said for me to do."

Ashley brought her voice down to a whisper and asked, "You brought up anal?"

Chelsea rolled her eyes and nodded her head yes. "Whatever, let's not talk about this. If it happens, it happens."

Ashley started to laugh. "All right, but for real, are you even prepared for something like that?"

The question tugged at her conscience. It felt like such a loaded question. "To be honest, I have no idea. I've never done it before."

"Oh my God, you've never done it before?"

"You have?"

Ashley didn't answer right away. It looked as though she was thinking about her answer first. Maybe she had suddenly become aware of how they were crossing into that area that they never crossed into together. "I did it a few times. It's rough at first, but once you get used to it you kind of even like it. That's all I'll say about that."

When Chelsea looked over at Jordan, he was putting the buns on the burgers and looking over at her. It was only for a split second before he looked away. There was something in the twinkle in his eye.

But she left that for later. The last thing that she wanted him to think of was for her to be impulsive. She wanted to keep her cool, play her cards right, and make it so that she had the upper hand.

That's exactly what she did during dinner. Everyone drank. Everyone ate the BBQ food that Jordan had cooked. It was a good time. But throughout that good time, Chelsea couldn't lie to herself. Jordan was giving her the eyes. There was this moment within her chest when she knew that everything was working. It was a tough pill to swallow because she couldn't believe it. She finally had his attention. After all this time, he was finally noticing her in the way that she had been hoping for so long.

It was after dinner when things got intense.

"So were you all talk or what?" Jordan asked as she threw out her plate. It was this intimate moment where it felt like it was just them. Even though everyone was laughing in the distance, the world kind of got quiet as he asked her that fateful question.

She found the courage to look him in the eyes. "Of course, I meant when I said. But are you man enough to take me? Because those are two very different things."

Jordan laughed, and she felt a little proud that she could get him to do that. He was a very stoic man even though he loved to party.

"Come up to my room." That was all he said before he walked away. She waited for a minute before she followed him into the house where they were going to do it. It was going to change her life forever. There was only one first time for that. And she was going to do it with Jordan. Would there be regrets? Time would tell. But of course, she had high hopes. This was what she wanted.

"I'm going inside," she said to Ashley on the way in.

Ashley held her arm and whispered, "Good luck. Hope your butt's clean."

Chelsea almost laughed until she realized that it was a real concern. Luckily she hadn't used the bathroom or anything that day. And she had taken a very thorough shower. She didn't want to think about things like that. She didn't want to sully the moment.

Chelsea wasted no time getting upstairs. She did her best to not imagine what was going to happen because that would only make her nervous. The anticipation was already enough for her.

When she opened the door to the room that Jordan would be staying in, he was sitting on the end of the bed picking at his thumb. He looked up with a smirk. "You aren't all talk. I'm shocked."

Chelsea shook her head and walked into the room. When she closed the door behind herself, it felt all real. Once again, the world had become a lot smaller. Everything outside that door didn't exist.

"I'm not all talk. I want you to have sex with me. I've been wanting that for a while."

Jordan wasted no time. He left the edge of the bed and walked up to Chelsea. Without any hesitation, he gave her a long kiss. Seventy-five percent of the way through the kiss, he slipped his tongue into her mouth.

The way that he kissed her involved him holding himself up against the door. This meant that both his arms were beside her head. He towered over her as well. All she wanted was for him to take her. She wanted to know when he was ready. This is exactly what she got. Because he slipped his hands underneath her armpits and lifted her to put her on the bed. It was like the fulfillment of all her dreams. At the same time, it was only the beginning.

Both his hands went to her breasts, giving them a little squeeze. They squished right out of the bra for a second. This made him want to lift the shirt and see what was underneath. This made her feel small in the best of ways. It's like she was being observed, studied, and picked apart. She was his prey.

"Take my shirt off," Chelsea said. She had never told someone to take her clothes off like that. It was an unprecedented situation, though. She no longer wanted to wear clothes. She wanted him to be observing her naked body. And that's exactly what he did.

Taking off her shirt, he ran his hands up and down her torso until he moved them to her back and unhooked her bra. Out flopped her double-D breasts. He grabbed one and ran his fingertip over the nipple.

The next thing he did was pull off her pants and underwear. They were yoga pants, so it wasn't that hard. She worried that she might soak the bed. She was so horny. He took the same fingertip from before and ran it up and down her clitoris. She melted in his presence. It was like she was some sort of guitar and he was a world-class musician.

His tongue went down there when he was done touching her. The thing flicked aggressively, more aggressively than his finger had gone. He was soaking up every inch of her, and she would have had it no other way.

"Are you ready?" he asked right before she climaxed.

It wasn't a hard question to understand. She knew exactly what he was alluding to. What he wanted to do. She couldn't believe that it was about to happen. "Yeah just go easy with me."

She couldn't remember whether or not she'd told him it was her first time. And she didn't want to seem like a scrub. So she just hoped for the best.

He put her in the doggy position. The only bad thing about that was she wanted to see what his dick looked, like but she couldn't facing the way she was.

Chelsea watched his shirt fly to the floor. Then she heard the zipper go down. That was when she turned around to sneak a peek. "I want to see it."

He laughed. Seconds later, out sprang his cock. It was fully erect, covered with veins, and kind of red, but long. After looking at it, she turned back around and closed her eyes. Never before had the focus been on her butthole so much. She could feel every bit of air on it.

When his penis touched the rim of her asshole, she flinched.

"You all right?" he asked.

Chelsea didn't know what she was feeling. All

she knew was that she didn't want to let him down, and she wanted to continue. "I'm great. Put it in."

He pushed his penis inside of her. At first, it felt like she was using the bathroom. And then it felt like pleasure.

In and out his penis went, and the more it happened, the more comfortable it became. She even enjoyed it.

Clutching the pillows, it felt like his penis was in her stomach. It was a feeling she had never experienced before. Never did she think she could get so much pleasure from his cock in her asshole. But that's exactly what was happening.

"Go harder," she said,

He didn't hesitate one bit.

The more he did it, the closer she felt like she was going to climax. It was downright unbelievable. She didn't think that it was possible to climax that way, especially on the first try. She did the math in her head. Maybe ten more pumps and she would come. She did the countdown in her head. Each pump was better than the last.

And then it happened.

She climaxed with a dick in her ass. She knew from that moment forward, she was going to do it again one day. Because she liked anal. Hopefully, Jordan had a good time just like she did.

Something told her that he did because he was finishing all over her back.

It was her happy ending.

Smack

by Calliope Barnes

She pressed the phone to her ear and used her free hand to stir the tomato sauce. Steam wafted and warmed the bridge of her nose as the smell of tomatoes and spices filled the air. Her stomach grumbled in response as she lifted the wooden spoon up to her lips and licked.

"Are you still listening?"

Geena sighed and set the phone down on the counter next to the stove. She placed it on speaker, crouched down, and turned down the stove. "I'm listening. Babe, I don't know what you want me to say."

Her best friend, Marisol Lopez, let out a deep sigh. "I don't know either."

"You could try talking to him," Geena suggested

with a quick look over at the phone. She took a few steps in the direction of the refrigerator and wrenched it open, white light spilling out onto the tile floors underneath her. "I know communication isn't his strong suit—"

"That's an understatement. If it's not about football, food, or sex, Mark doesn't want to hear it," Marisol replied with another sigh. "I honestly don't know what to do anymore."

Geena reached into the fridge and pushed aside a few containers. "You really should talk to him, Mar. Hopefully, if the two of you sit down and have a heart-to-heart, you'll clear the air."

"You mean like you and Paul have heart-to-hearts?"

Geena blushed. "It works for us."

"Uh-huh. I can hear the excitement in your voice. You're planning something for tonight, aren't you?"

"He's been busy with work all week, and I've barely seen him," Geena replied with a quick look over her shoulders at the living room window overlooking the driveway. "So, yeah, I've got some plans for us tonight."

And they all involved him walking in from work, seeing her in nothing but an apron, and letting his briefcase clatter to the floor. Her heart jumped into her throat at the thought. Then she gave a slight shake of her head and kicked the refrigerator door shut with the back of her leg.

A shiver raced up her spine.

Outside the window, the wind howled, and a few snowflakes swirled. Geena shivered again before snatching her fluffy robe off the counter and turning up the heat. She waited a few moments before returning to the stove and switching it off completely. When she was done, she chopped up a few vegetables and tossed them into the bowl.

Geena surveyed the candles set up in the living room, on the kitchen counter and leading up to the bedroom, where rose petals were thrown onto the king sized bed. She lifted the phone up to her ear, murmured something to Marisol, and ended the call. Once she did, she heard Paul's car pull up in the driveway.

His door opened and slammed shut a moment later.

Her lips lifted into a smile as she cast a quick look in the oven at the roasted chicken and switched off. Hastily, she removed her robe, tossed it onto one of the high-top chairs pressed against the counter, and pressed both hands on her hips.

A heartbeat later, the front door clicked open, and Paul stepped in, a strong gust of wind pouring in behind him. He kicked the door shut with the back of his leg and unwound the scarf from around his neck. Slowly, he kicked his shoes off and left them by the door.

"Honey, I'm home."

"I'm here," Geena replied in a low voice. "How was work?"

"You know how the end of the quarter is," Paul responded without looking at her. He shrugged out of his coat and hung it up behind the door. Then his hands moved to his collar, brushing off the flakes there. "They're really busting my ass."

Geena took a few steps forward and flashed him a smile. "I bet I can make it better."

Paul raked a hand through his hair. "You already do, so what's for...." He twisted to face her, the rest of his sentence dying on his lips. Paul opened and closed his mouth several times, but nothing came out. Finally, his briefcase fell to the floor with a thud, and he strode toward her.

"What's for what?"

"I was going to ask what's for dinner," Paul told her, coming to a stop a few feet away. His eyes raked over her, from the top of her head down to the tips of her toes and back up again. "But I can see I don't need to."

"Dinner is in the oven," Geena breathed, bridging the gap between him and wrapping her arms around his torso. "This is dessert."

Paul placed both hands on her waist and squeezed. "I think I want to start with dessert."

Geena pushed herself up on the tips of her toes and pressed her lips to his. Paul growled against her mouth and pushed himself against her. She raised her fingers up to his shoulders and threaded them through his hair. Then she gave him a firm squeeze, earning another low growl. Without warning, Paul's hands moved down to her waist, and he hoisted her up so her legs were locked around him.

Her heart thundered against her chest as he carried her inside. "You don't want a drink first?"

Paul paused in the doorway to their room and kissed her hard. "I only want you."

With that, he stepped into the room and set her down on the mattress. When his hands moved to his clothes, Geena sat up on her knees and reached for him. Wordlessly, her fingers moved over the buttons, undoing one after the other in quick succession. The shirt fell to the floor with a flutter, revealing tanned and smooth skin underneath.

Geena's breath hitched in her throat as she climbed off the bed and knelt down on the carpeted floor so she was at eye level with his waist. Paul's dark eyes watched her intently, beads of sweat forming on his forehead. Her lips lifted into a smirk as she undid his belt and pulled his pants down over his knees, letting it pool around his ankles. With a grunt, Paul stepped out of the pants and kicked them away.

She palmed him over his boxers and glanced up at him. "Someone is excited."

Paul's hands moved to the back of her head and squeezed. "Someone definitely is."

Abruptly, Paul drew her up to her feet and crushed her to him.

As soon as his mouth touched hers, something in her unfurled, hot and demanding. It slithered through her as he twisted his arms behind her back and fumbled with the knot at her neck. He muttered something into her mouth before wrenching his lips away. He stared at her through hooded eyes, panting with desire. Then he ripped the apron away from her and tossed it over his head.

"That was my favorite apron," Geena told him with a pout.

"I'll get you a new one," Paul said, his voice

thick and low. He shifted so their bodies were pressed together, heaving and glistening with sweat. Paul took both of her arms and wrapped them around his neck. Once he moved, her knees hit the back of the bed, and she fell backwards. Immediately, he climbed on top of her, his lips descending onto hers.

Rough and demanding.

Like he couldn't get enough of her.

His hands moved up and down her sides, leaving a trail of heat in their wake.

Geena moaned when his hands moved to her ears, tugging on her lobes. He kicked her legs apart and settled them in between, inches away from her center. With a whimper, Geena sat up and pushed Paul, so he was flat on his back. Her eyes didn't leave his face as she knelt down, so she was at eye level with his hard, glistening member.

She gave Paul a smile before her tongue darted out and licked. "I love how big you are, Paul."

Paul's hips flexed and he growled, "Yeah? Do you like it when I'm in your mouth?"

Geena nodded and took him into her mouth, pausing when she reached the hilt. She kept her eyes on his face as he moved, watching as he bucked underneath her. When he cupped the back of her neck and squeezed, another wave of molten hot desire burst through her.

All she could see was him.

And all she could hear was the sound of his heavy breathing filling the room.

By the light of the candles and the thin sliver of the moon, she watched him, a familiar feeling inside of her chest swelling as she did. When his hands moved to her breasts, palming and kneading the nipples there, her pulse quickened.

He was completely at her mercy and enjoying every minute of it.

She loved seeing this side of him.

Suddenly, Paul pressed his lips firmly to hers. As soon as she drew back, he gave her a slow, sultry smile that had her heart stopping in her chest. "I want to finish inside of you."

Geena licked her lips and swallowed. "Okay."

She fell back onto the mattress and spread her legs apart. Paul crawled forward, his chest rising and falling unevenly as he loomed over her. Then he placed one hand on either side of her and positioned himself at her entrance. He lowered his head, took one nipple in between his teeth, and tugged. A jolt coursed through her as one hand moved between them and darted in between her wet folds.

He added another finger and stroked.

Geena threw her head back and moaned. "Oh, Paul. Oh, yes."

"You're so wet for me, baby," Paul said into her skin. He moved to the other nipple and bit, sending dual waves of pain and pleasure ricocheting through her. "I can't wait to fuck you."

Geena fixed her gaze on him and blew out a breath. "What are you waiting for?"

He glanced down at her, and in one quick move, he eased himself in. Geena held herself still as her hand moved over the length of his back and paused at his ass. She gave it a firm squeeze, and he bucked against her.

Paul lifted her arms up over her head and held them in a vise-like grip. "You're mine, Geena."

Geena wriggled and writhed against him. "I'm yours."

Paul eased out of her and slammed back in. "Say it again."

"I'm yours," Geena repeated in a thick voice. "Only yours."

Paul brought his head to a rest against the headboard and circled his hips. "You're so fucking tight and wet. Fuck, I don't know how long I'm going to last."

Geena ground against him. "We're just getting started."

Paul lifted his head up and looked at her, and the muscles in her stomach tightened. "God, I love how excited you are."

Geena linked her legs over his waist, drawing him closer. "I've been craving this all week."

Paul groaned and buried his face in her neck.

He placed hot, wet kisses down the side of her face and her neck. Quickly, he withdrew his lips and grazed the sensitive skin there. Geena tossed her head to the side and squeezed her eyes shut. Paul sank his teeth into her skin, and she hissed.

Holy shit.

Even after all this time, he still knew exactly where to touch her.

And how.

He knew exactly what to do to have her sweating and begging for more.

Her release came quickly, exploding through her as she writhed and spasmed underneath him. When her eyes flew open, white spots danced in her field of vision, and her chest burned with effort. Little by little, Paul's face came back into focus, and her hands fell to her sides. She pushed her hair out of her eyes and gave Paul a bright smile.

In one quick move, she had him on his back and placed one leg on either side of him. "My turn."

Paul's fingers dug into her waist. "I love it when you take control."

Geena lowered her head and kissed his chest, moving from the smattering of hair there to his neck, and the sensitive spot underneath his ear. She nipped the skin there, and Paul bucked against her, his hot breath sending a swarm of butterflies to her stomach.

Paul gripped her waist and thrust into her. "Fuck. Yes, baby. Ride me."

Geena straightened her back, placing her palms on either side of her, and her hands moved to her breasts. Paul's eyes widened as he watched her play with herself, rivulets of sweat sliding down her back and sides. His hips rose up off the mattress and slammed into her, sending another shock through her system.

She threw her head back and moaned. "God, you feel so good."

Paul kept one hand on her waist, and the other slid up her back and cupped the back of her neck. He shifted so she fell forward, and he took one nipple between his mouth. Geena placed her hands on the headboard and released a deep, shaky breath.

His hands moved back to her ass and squeezed.

Geena brought her head to a rest against the headboard and squeezed her eyes shut. Paul moved to the other breast, sucking and biting until they were both as hard as pebbles. Her heart pounded against her chest as she bounced up and down, bringing them both closer and closer to the edge. Suddenly, Paul withdrew his hands, and a jolt went through her when he smacked her.

She froze and leaned back to look at him.

Paul's eyes cleared as he looked at her, a myriad of emotions dancing across his face. "Why did you stop?"

With a slight shake of her head, Geena moved again, all too aware of the stinging sensation on her backside. Still, she ground against him and laced her fingers through his. He buried his face in the crook of her neck, and she inhaled, catching the scent of sandalwood and lavender. Paul eased in and out of her, pushing himself farther and farther each time until he filled every inch of her.

Yet it wasn't enough.

Geena wanted more.

Needed more.

She threw her head back and stared at him through hooded eyes, his bottom lip drawn between his teeth and a furrow between his brows. He rubbed his hands up and down her back, leaving goosebumps in his wake. Then his hands moved to her breasts, pressing them together. Everywhere he touched, every inch of skin burned and blazed, and Geena couldn't tell where he began and she ended.

Her pulse quickened as another wave of desire built up within her.

This time when she came, she rode out her high, bucking and thrashing on top of him as she did. The bed dipped and creaked underneath their weight as wave after wave of desire raced through her. As soon as her breathing evened out, she used the back of her hand to wipe the sweat off her face.

With a smile, she climbed off of Paul and twisted so her back was to him.

In the closet mirror across from her, she saw Paul scramble to his feet and position himself behind her. He stroked her behind, pressed a kiss to the small of her back, and thrust into her. Slowly, Geena moved against him and groaned.

Over and over, he eased out and slammed back into her.

In the glass, she saw his muscles ripple, and he dug his nails into her waist. When his eyes met hers in the mirror, her heart jumped into her throat. He gave her a look that made her insides quiver. Then he brought his head to a rest against the curve of her back and thrust.

Together, they moved, taking and giving in equal pleasure while they inched closer and closer to oblivion. Geena kept her eyes open the entire time, unable to look away. She kept imaging his hand smacking her behind, and it filled her with a strange yearning in the center of her chest.

She closed one eye and kept the other open, admiring Paul's powerful muscles as he slammed in and out of her. One hand stayed on the small of her back, and the other darted forward and stroked her sensitive bud. Then it moved to her nipple, pinching and pulling. He moved to the other nipple when her breasts began to harden.

With a smirk, Paul's hand darted in between her wet folds and stroked the sensitive bundle of nerves. As soon as he found her sweet spot, his movements changed and grew frantic, moving with wild abandon. Both eyes fluttered closed, and she ground against him, pulse hammering in her ears.

A short while later, she came undone, panting and writhing as she did.

Paul gave a few more thrusts before he shot his load into her and grew still. His head came to a rest against her back, his hot breath leaving goosebumps in its wake. Slowly, he eased out of her and fell backward onto the mattress. A heartbeat later, Geena collapsed against him, bringing her head to a rest in the center of his chest, over the pounding of his heart.

He draped an arm over her shoulders and squeezed. "That was amazing."

Geena pressed a kiss to his throat. "It was."

Paul tilted her chin up using his thumb and forefinger and looked into her eyes. "About earlier, I'm sorry if I got carried away—"

Geena pressed a finger to her lips. "Don't be. I was just surprised."

Paul's lips spread into a smile. "You liked it?"

"I loved it," Geena whispered, pausing to press a kiss to his lips. "I would actually love to try it again."

Paul chuckled and kissed her. "You got it, baby.".

Going Pro on Your First Time
by Randall Kim-Collins

I'm NOT sure where to start with this. Maybe it's because the whole experience has been one mind-blowing event after the other. Or maybe it's just the fact that I feel so fucking good, and I have no idea why I haven't done this earlier.

Well, actually, I do know why. High school girls, with their Instagram personas and flashy fakeness mixed with an unhealthy cocktail of emotions, hormones and Daddy issues probably aren't the best when it comes to your "first time." You're either too weird for the cheerleaders who rarely know what's good for them, too dull for the popular ones who have a reputation to uphold, or too brother-like for the rest who are just trying to find their way in this world. You're a shadow in the back of the class, half-asleep and half wondering why the hell anyone would choose to keep learning after twelve years of hell.

But, hey, as the son of a lawyer and a pediatrician, there really isn't any discussion about what comes after school, right? UCLA, here I come. One more steppingstone on my way to the big, bad world of debt, meaningless relationships, and anti-depressants. My brother says things change once you walk into those dorm rooms, and I'd like to believe it, but he's rarely had to put up with half the shit I've been through. Nah, Josh was always the one who knew how to get what he wanted, and when it came to the ladies, I think he holds the record for most panties collected in a year.

I think that's why finding out I was still a virgin pissed him off more than anything. What did he say? *No brother of mine is going to UCLA without having wet his rod?* I can hardly remember half the shit he says, especially when it came to making me feel uncomfortable and stroking that damn ego of his.

But he did have a point. Josh Harland was a ladies' man, a god among men, and a conqueror of pussy. Derek Harland, on the other hand, only held the highest score for most times humiliated in the cafeteria.

"We're going to get this right, Derek," I remember Josh saying. "Give me two days, and we'll get this all sorted out!"

Thing is, I didn't really want to get anything sorted out. Sure, the notion of going to uni a virgin didn't thrill me, but I had a feeling I could make it work. There was always a place for guys like me who could get by with *I was waiting for the right person* without having to worry about being ridiculed. Besides, was I really missing out on anything? I always thought I was fine.

But after last night, boy was I wrong!

It started with a night out with the boys, as Josh likes to call it. Every time he's in town, he has to gather up the entire gang and basically barhop across the city. This time, he dragged me along with him, and although I hate his band of thieves, it was kind of refreshing to get out. Packing and organizing were two things I wasn't very good at, and the fact that my mother *was* made it just as bad. You try spending hours with an OCD doctor making sure my socks and underwear weren't in the same bags.

Our first stop was a place called Bentley's, a bar

frequented by most of the city's younger crowd because the owner didn't care much for checking IDs. I think he's been fined more times than I can count, and there was a period when he had to close completely, but I guess it's the Irish rebel inside him. Or maybe he knows the young ones don't know what's good for them and usually end up drinking the bar dry.

By the first hour, my brother and his friends were already tipsy and loud, and it was a struggle to keep a smile on my face despite the glares we were getting from everyone. I wasn't allowed to drink; designated driver and all. Which made the whole thing a little bit of a doozy. I mean, it's not a lot of fun being the sober one in the midst of a pack of drunken hyenas, but I wasn't complaining. I needed a few hours out of the house.

By the third bar, I was doing everything I could to keep my brother from falling over. And there were still two more bars on the list.

"I think we should call it a night," I said to Josh, but he just waved me away and pushed me into the driver's seat.

"The Mayday!" he yelled.

That made me hesitate. The Mayday was a little too chic for the drunk mob I was driving around, and my father frequented the place a lot. It was a quaint little place in a family-owned hotel lobby. The regulars rubbed shoulders with some pretty big names, and the owner of the hotel was one of my dad's clients. I didn't think this would be a great idea at all.

"How about we head home?" I asked.

"Mayday, now!" came the reply.

I reluctantly obliged.

On our way, we had to stop to drop off party members who had had enough for the night, as expressed by their vomit in the back seat, and by the time we reached The Mayday, it was just me and Josh.

"We can turn back home," I said. "You made it this far, man, you're good."

"No!" Josh slurred. "This is the most important stop!" He leaned over and smiled. "Besides, I booked us a room for the night. We're going to live it up!"

"Josh, please," I sighed. "I need to air out the damn car and get it cleaned in the morning. We don't need to spend the night." Besides, I knew he was probably just going to pass out and I was going to have to try to sleep while enduring his snores.

"Just go," he said, stumbling out of the car. "I need to make a stop at the bar and then I'll meet you upstairs."

We split up in the lobby, with Josh swaying as he walked to the bar and me holding the card key he had palmed me before smacking my back and wishing me luck. I took the elevator to the third floor, stepped out into a moderately well-decorated floor and tried to find our room. I cursed the fact that the night was ending like this but found some solace in knowing that at least for tonight, I didn't have to worry about carrying my brother into the house without waking our parents.

The room was pretty sweet, come to think of it. The bathroom was huge, with a stand-in shower and what looked like a Jacuzzi. A huge desk occupied one corner, and a window wall looked out to a pretty awesome view of the park. There was a huge mirror on the ceiling above the only problem I had with the room: a single Queen-sized bed.

My stomach lurched at the idea of sharing a bed with my drunk brother.

The knock on the door startled me, and I was already working up a slur of curses to throw at Josh. But it wasn't my brother waiting when I opened it.

She was gorgeous.

Brunette hair tied back in a high ponytail, green eyes looking at me from behind thick bangs, and lips colored in a shade of maroon that was just captivating. Her skin screamed expensive care routine, and the blue dress clinging to her body left very little to the imagination. She smiled at me, and something inside me flipped.

"Derek?"

I could only nod, and it made her smile wider.

"Your brother said you'd be here. I'm Leya."

I pursed my lips and nodded. My mouth had suddenly gone very dry.

She giggled. "Can I come in?"

She didn't wait for an answer, pushing me gently to one side while floating past me, and I closed the door.

With her back to me, she dropped her clutch on the chair by the desk and looked out the window wall. "It really is a beautiful view."

I coughed and cleared my throat. "Yeah," I croaked. "It's really something, um, Le..."

She turned around and gave me a half-smile. "Forgot my name already?"

She walked up to me, put one hand on my chest, and used the other one to comb the hair out of my eyes. "You're cute, I'll give you that." She leaned in and kissed me, and I breathed her in, waves of electricity shooting through my body. She broke away and stared at me, green eyes like emeralds.

"Sorry," I whispered.

"It's Leya," she said, guiding me to the bed and pushing me gently down so I was sitting in front of her. "Don't worry. By the end of tonight, you'll remember it."

"I don't..." I stopped as she slowly dropped one strap from her shoulder and then the other. "I don't understand."

The dress dropped to the floor, and the nakedness that greeted me made me hard in an instant. She was perfect, a Greek goddess chiseled to perfection. Her breasts seemed to shine in the warm light of the room, the necklace with its pendant nestled between them nicely. Her body curved inwards to her waist, then out again into long, beautiful legs. She was shaved clean except for a small patch shaped like a triangle, pointing to where I needed to go, as if I needed directions.

"I hear you're going off to college," she said, slowly straddling me, eyes fixed on mine, breasts inches from my mouth.

"University," I whispered.

She raised her eyebrows. "Oh, an educated man." She kissed my cheek, then my neck, and I swear I could have come right then and there. "Consider me a going away present. Your brother said you needed a little...assistance."

I swallowed hard when her hand snaked down to my crotch and squeezed an already ready-to-burst hard-on. "Did he?"

"Don't worry, Derek," she said, kissing my neck, my jawline, my earlobe. Her breath was hot against my ear. "I'll take good care of you."

When she kissed me again, I returned the kiss with vigor. Her lips were luscious, and the way she gripped the back of my neck, the way her hips slowly began to grind against me, unleashed an animalistic need inside me like I had never felt before. This goddess was here for me, and all my disdain for the night, all my anger towards Josh, dissipated immediately.

My hands found her hips and held tight as she continued grinding against my crotch. She kissed me hungrily, and the heat inside me grew to a burning inferno. She pulled back and guided me to her breasts, and I took one soft nipple after the other into my mouth. I sucked on them hungrily, even biting gently.

"Easy, tiger," she whispered. "Nice and slow now."

Her instructions meant little to me. My hands reached up behind her and pulled her to me, my mind blown that I was even doing this. She gripped me by the hair and pushed my face closer, as if wanting me to swallow her entire breast. She ground harder against me as I sucked. I tried biting again, softer this time, and was rewarded with a satisfied moan.

I pulled off my shirt, and she pushed me back, expertly getting rid of my belt and unbuttoning my jeans. She used her teeth to pull down the zipper, and I shuddered when her fingers scratched against my abs and she pulled my jeans off.

"Let's get the first one out of the way," she said with a wink. She was already pulling down my boxers.

"The first what?"

She giggled. "Don't worry, handsome, I know what I'm doing." She looked down at my erection, then back at me with a smile. "Trust me."

I didn't need goading. Her fingers wrapped around my cock and her lips found the inside of my side, kissing their way up as she squeezed. I could have sworn the world around me had exploded, and I was floating dead somewhere in space, my mind lost in an abyss of emotions I had never felt before. I looked down, met her eyes, and clutched the sheets tightly when her tongue took a long lick from the root to the tip of my cock. I sucked in a deep breath and almost lost my mind when I felt her lips devour me, my cock deep in the warmth of her mouth.

Her hand pumped slowly, her tongue twirled, and I lost myself in her sucking. This must have been what Josh meant when he said the right woman can literally blow you away. I pulsed in her mouth as her head bobbed up and down. She cupped my balls and massaged them, her other hand stroking me like a metronome in perfect sync. My entire body burned in heat, and my muscles clenched in the tell-tale sign of a man about to cum hard.

She sensed I was close, took me out of her mouth, and pressed my cock against her breast. That soft, beautiful mound of flesh, her nipple hard against me as her hand pumped. I couldn't hold back any longer, and with a loud grunt, I exploded. I came so hard, I saw bright spots flashing behind my closed eyes. She squeezed, stroking me at a slower pace, milking me for all I was worth, and I could have sworn the room was spinning.

"That's number one," Leya said. I looked down at her, and she smiled wickedly at me, a woman who knew exactly what she was doing and obviously reveled in the power she had over a virgin boy like me.

She was right.

She knew exactly what she was doing.

Grabbing my boxers, she wiped the cum off her hand and breasts, then tossed it away. She crawled onto the bed, kissing my abs, my side, my chest, and finally my neck. Her breasts brushed against my chest, and the heat coming from her crotch was like a furnace against my cock. She might have had a magical hold on me, but it was clear she was just as excited. The power, maybe. The fact that for tonight, although she was my present, I was her toy.

"Now that that's out of the way," Leya said. I grabbed her hard when she pushed her pussy down against me, her lips enveloping my cock, her wetness burning around me. She began to grind her hips again, my cock sliding up and down her pussy. "Let's get the most out of our time together."

She sat up, her majestic breasts even more impressive when she pushed them together, her hips grinding harder as she picked up the pace. She let her ponytail loose, and waves of gorgeous, brown hair cascaded down her shoulders. Smiling at me and biting her lip, she slowed her pace down, moved her hips up, and smiled even wider when she slid my cock inside her and I caught my breath.

"You feel good, University," she teased.

She felt fucking incredible. She didn't move, just sat there, clenching her pussy muscles around me and relaxing them in a perfect rhythm that would have had me blowing my load in a second if I hadn't come already. Then she began to move, up and down, slowly at first so I could feel every bit of her. She continued to do this, driving me insane, and then began to pick up the pace. She leaned back, grinding hard and fast against me, her breasts bouncing and her head thrown back. I closed my eyes and lost myself in the frenzy, electricity shooting up and down my body.

She fell forward, pushing one nipple into my mouth as I grabbed her ass. She rode me like I was a stallion, her hips bouncing up and down, slamming me into her hot pussy so hard her moans turned into screams. She smothered me with her breasts and suddenly began to grind hard and fast against me. I felt like I was ready to come again, and I squeezed her ass hard as I tried to hold back.

"Not yet," she gasped. "Not yet. I want you to fuck me before you come."

She rolled off me and onto her back, pulling me

to her and kissing me with an animalistic lust I easily matched.

"Fuck me, Derek," Leya moaned. "I know you have it in you. Come on!"

She opened her legs and guided my cock to her pussy, and I pushed into her with such ease, it was like I had done this a thousand times before. She arched her back, laughing. "My God, I knew this would be worth it!" she screamed.

I pulled out and slammed inside her, pulled out and slammed in, out and in, copying what she did to me, slow and hard at first then picking up the tempo. I could already feel my balls screaming for release, but the way her nails dug into my back, the way her legs wrapped around my waist, I was going to die before giving up on an opportunity like this.

So I fucked her. Just like she asked. Just like she demanded. Just like she screamed at me to do. I don't know if she was paid to do this or not, but I didn't care. Her moans echoed in the room, and her hips pushed up against me with every thrust I did. I was like a jackhammer, slamming my cock into her so hard, I had a split second of worry that I might hurt either one of us. But she just wanted more.

She had me pressed against, legs wrapped tight

around my waist, breasts crushed between us, her hot breath against my ear driving me to the edge.

"You're close, aren't you?" she moaned. "You're close, baby, I can feel it."

"I am..." My muscles tightened.

She pushed me off her and onto my back, grabbing my cock and pumping. "Here's another little trick for you." She smiled mischievously, then took me into her mouth and sucked hard.

I couldn't hold back any longer and instantly exploded, my hands grabbing her head as I lifted my hips and pushed deeper into her mouth. Thinking about it now, I could have choked her, the idiot that I was. But at that moment, I didn't care. All I was thinking of was how the hell could a man have an orgasm like this and not black out?

I collapsed on the bed, my heart pounding in my chest, my breathing as fast as if I had just run a marathon. I closed my eyes, my head spinning, and felt Leya move off the bed. Somewhere in the distance, there was the click of a light switch followed by the sound of running water. I wanted to check on her, see if she needed anything, but I was just too tired to move.

A few minutes later, I felt her crawl into the bed again, and her soft body wrapped itself around me. I felt her lips against my neck, her breath calm and steady. Her fingers stroked my cock softly, as if thanking it for a good job.

I turned to look at her. "You don't have to go?" I asked.

Her eyes met mine, and she smiled. "Your brother's booked me for the night," she said. "For the next few hours, I'm all yours."

I made good use of those hours.

The Pastor's Daughter
by Paulette Marsh

IT WAS strange talking to a pastor when she had such thoughts. They were thoughts that didn't align with the church. But she had them anyway. And maybe, just maybe he could help her to find herself without any judgment.

Thirty-year-old Vivian was a lesbian. Her ex-husband, who had just divorced her, had no idea. And he would probably never know because they were no longer in contact. He didn't like the fact that she no longer wanted sex. She completely understood that. But was the world ready to know why? That was the real question.

"Why do you think that intimacy fled you?" Pastor Jenkins asked her while they sat in the empty church. They did this every Friday night after she got off work from her job. She worked in telemarketing. She was a supervisor, one of the top ones. It was a fulfilling job at times, it was just that her personal life always got in the way of everything else.

"I don't think that I'm attracted to him anymore. I think I lost that attraction," she said without revealing that she was a lesbian. How she was going to do that, she had no idea. She knew what the church's stance was on lesbianism. Although it had become more accepting of gays, she was still worried. She had built such a rapport with him over the last couple of weeks, she didn't want anything ruining that.

"You know, in a marriage, there's a lot more to it than just attraction. Something else had to shift inside of you. And after all these weeks of talking, I still feel as though we haven't touched the surface of what that may be. And I'm afraid you're not going to be able to move forward with your life, God's life, if you can't accept what he's filled you with."

It was on the tip of her tongue and yet, she couldn't do it. She couldn't reveal that she was gay. There wasn't one person in the world that knew, but there was one animal that did. It was her cat. Her cat only knew because she would watch gay porn. Then she apologized to God. She knew pornography was not something that anyone should be into. But it was her outlet. It was her way of coming out without coming out.

"Sometimes, Pastor Jenkins, I feel like the world is not ready for my reasoning."

"Oh, so you know? Do you have something in mind?"

Lesbian. That single word came to her mind. There was no avoiding it. It was there. It was flashing like a neon sign in Vegas. No matter where she looked, there was no looking away from it.

"I don't know. Sometimes I think I know and sometimes I don't."

It was then that they both heard footsteps coming from the back of the church.

Pastor Jenkins was always super calm; he didn't even look behind himself to see who it was. But Vivian did.

And when she did, she saw someone with the opposite complexion of herself. It was a pale blonde. But she wasn't pale in a bad way. She was pale in a beautiful way. Almost like porcelain skin.

The woman was downright angelic. It was fitting almost. The closer she got, Vivian saw it. She saw the gay pride T-shirt. There was no way not to recognize that rainbow. And something told Vivian that she wasn't just representing. She was part of the community.

When Pastor Jenkins finally turned around, his face lit up like the same sign that was in her head, and he said, "Tia. There you are. Vivian, this is my daughter Tia."

Pastor Jenkins had a gay daughter. It was almost comical to her. She had spent weeks pretending that she wasn't gay out of fear of his judgment. And yet, his very own daughter was a lesbian.

"Oh wow, it's so nice to meet you. I've been speaking to your father for a few weeks now. He's helped me through my divorce."

Tia raised an eyebrow. For whatever reason, Vivian found it to be sexy. It was the subtle movement, the nuances, that drove Vivian crazy just looking at her. "Well, my father is a great man to talk to. He's wise beyond his years. I was just giving him this book back."

Tia handed her father a book and then sent her attention back to Vivian. Vivian was taken aback by her strong gaze. "What do you say you and I go for coffee? I feel like someone who just got out of a divorce needs a new friend."

Vivian lost her breath at the thought.

"That would be a splendid idea if you ask me,"

Jenkins said. "If I know anything about Vivian, all she does is work and go home. She could use someone to hang out with from time to time."

Tia smiled and hugged her father. "I live right up the block from the church," she said to Vivian. "So don't think that I walked a million miles to drop this book off to my dad even though I would have if I needed to."

They all chuckled. "You don't seem like a crazy person, don't worry," Vivian added.

"Well, you two get on your way. I have some studying in the back to do. Feel free to stop at any time, Vivian. You know I'm always here."

Vivian smiled at Jenkins and then left with Tia. The second that they started to walk off with one another, Vivian got goosebumps.

When they were out of the church, Tia said, "You got divorced because you're a lesbian, huh?"

Vivian's cheeks went red. Her tongue went dry. She lost the ability to speak for a good three seconds. "I don't know what you're talking about," she finally blurted out nervously.

Tia laughed. "No, please. I know a lesbian when I see one. The divorce just confirmed it for me. Why do you feel the need to hide it from the world? Are you still lying to yourself?"

"No." Vivian was shocked by how quickly she said it.

"Okay, so you're worried about the rest of the world. Why? Do you have shame about being a lesbian?"

Her throat went even drier. She didn't think that was possible. "I don't have shame about it. I don't know why I hide it."

"Do you feel like you can't come out until you feel like you have an anchor, something that will validate your desire?"

Vivian stayed quiet.

"Wait a minute...You've never actually been with a woman. You're afraid that you're going to be with a woman and not like it so you won't allow yourself to say that you're a lesbian."

Once again, Vivian's throat went even drier. She couldn't believe it. She had been quantified, summed up, and figured out, all in a matter of a couple of minutes.

Tia stopped walking and stood in front of Vivian. She took both of Tia's hands and held them in hers. "Oh my God. Sweetheart. There is a reason I dropped that book off today. And it's to save your ass."

Vivian laughed and took her hands back. "How are you going to save me?"

"I'm right out of a breakup. You're right out of a divorce. You've also never been with a woman. And I'm freaking horny."

Vivian laughed again, but this time her cheeks went red once more. "I can't believe I'm having this conversation with anyone." She started to walk, not knowing where she was going. It was all from nerves.

Tia ran up to her. "Come on now, don't be bashful. I saw the way you looked at me when I walked into the church. Let me be your first. And I'll prove to you that you're a lesbian."

"You know, for the daughter of a pastor, you're aggressive. I don't know what the word is."

"Gay? I just believe in things happen for a reason. I can tell that you're struggling. I can tell that you need someone to push you in the right direction. And as an openly gay woman, I know how hard it can be to not be an openly gay woman because I was one of the latter for a very long time. And no one should have to suffer through that. You know what I mean?"

Vivian found herself getting oddly emotional. Her eyes even began to water. "Whatever. Let's have dinner.

And then I'll decide what I want to do. I appreciate you opening up to me, okay? I know I may sound ungrateful and cold, but it's only because I'm not used to having these discussions. You're the only one in this world who has pegged me for a lesbian. And it's not easy to just suddenly talk about this stuff. It may be easier for you because you've had more practice than I have."

Tia folded her arms and nodded. "I understand that completely. I remember when I was first in your position. It feels like I have verbal constipation in a way. I promise you, once you get over that hump, it becomes a lot easier. Especially in the day and age that we live in. If this were the '80s or something, I don't know how this conversation would be going right now. But I know all the places in this world where you and I aren't weird. And I also promise you that when you stand before me, you're not weird either."

Vivian smiled. "You know, aside from realizing that you were gay, I also realized that your father had rubbed off on you and your ability to connect with people."

Tia laughed. "Yes, I would not be good at communicating without my dad. All of my emotions would be stifled. Luckily I have him. He's always been a guiding light in my life. I don't know what I'd do without him. But where do you want to eat?"

The thought excited Vivian. The last time she had been on a real date with someone who she wasn't married to was years ago. But at the same time, she just wanted something simple; something down to earth. "Let's go to Applebee's. I love Applebee's."

Tia laughed in an endearing way. "I like how simple you are. There are no bells and whistles. What you see is what you get."

"Are you saying that I look simple?"

Tia laughed again and gave Vivian the eye. "Have you ever received a real compliment from a woman? I'm not just talking about a sweater or earrings. I'm talking about have you ever heard a woman tell you what she really feels about you?"

Vivian's heart began to race. She wasn't sure whether or not things were really going to happen. Was she really going to indulge in her lesbian desires for once? Was there's really going to be no red tape around that? It could be. There was nothing stopping her.

"I've never heard anything like that, no. But I'm willing to."

"Well, I think you're a beautiful and sexy woman. I know that's how curious your eyes were the first time I saw them. And then I looked down at your breasts. Up to your lips. And even from a distance, from across that church, I wanted to kiss them."

Vivian couldn't remember the last time she'd had a racing heart like this. It was beating out of her chest. It was giving her goosebumps and adrenaline all at the same time. "What's stopping you from doing so?"

For the first time in public, with nothing hiding her, a woman kissed her. And that woman's name was Tia.

Her lips were soft, and she was aggressive. Their tongues played a beautiful song together. When she pulled off, Vivian could say only one thing. "I don't want Applebee's anymore. I want you."

They wound up in Tia's apartment. The kisses that they were sharing made the one on the street look amateur.

Vivian couldn't believe that after so many years of fantasizing about being with a woman, it had finally come to fruition. It was all really happening.

She was kissing a woman. She was feeling her body, grabbing her ass over her jeans, squeezing her titties over her shirt. There was no doubt that those clothes were going to come off in a few seconds. But it was Vivian's clothes that came off first.

Tia wasted no time and took her shirt off. And then her bra, freeing her medium-sized titties. Tia's eyes had a party. She licked one, caressing the nipple with her tongue.

"Never had a woman lick your titty before, huh?" Tia asked.

"You're the first, baby."

That made Tia suck on it. It surprised her how aggressive Tia could be. In turn, it made Vivian want to be aggressive too. For a while, Tia sucked on her titty, and Vivian squeezed hers. She even ventured lower and caressed her vagina over the pants.

"Why don't you take my pants off and really feel it?"

Once again, Vivian's heart raced out of her chest. But that didn't stop her from sitting up and unbuttoning Tia's jeans. Then came the zipper. She could see the little lace of Vivian's panties beneath. She couldn't believe it. This was really happening.

She clutched the band of both the jeans and the underwear and pulled them down. When she did, she saw Vivian's shaved pussy. There was not a hair on it. The hood was more prominent than hers. Vivian liked it. It was the first vagina she had seen up close that wasn't hers. She gave it one swipe and finally considered herself a real lesbian. But it was time to take it up a notch as well. She started to lick. She had never tasted it before. Even with herself, she'd never dared to try it. She liked the flavor, though. It made her want more and more. And even made her go into the vagina with her fingers. There was something special about feeling Tia's insides. She felt every inch of her. It felt like there were ridges on top of her vagina on the inside. Touching that made Tia's eyes close. It also made her mouth open.

Seeing all that happen drove Vivian to go a little faster and harder. She also wanted to see what Tia's titties looked like. So she stopped for a moment and removed the rest of Tia's clothes. Her breasts were very small. The bra had made them look bigger. It almost felt like Vivian had stumbled upon a little secret. It turned her on, and she got to share that secret with Tia. Despite the sides, she still sucked on them.

"First time for everything," she said while rubbing her other breast.

As Vivian sucked on her titty, she still fingered Tia. And then she realized something crazy, something that she hadn't expect to happen for quite some time. Her body started to stiffen. It meant that she was going to climax.

"Oh my God." Tia's eyes looked at Vivian's for a moment. "Holy shit, Vivian, really? You're really good."

Seconds later, Tia stopped moving for a moment and squeezed the sheets underneath her hands. Her face was a mask of pleasure. It was a totally different look than what she'd worn regularly. Vivian took great pride in the fact that she could morph like that. It was a sense of accomplishment that she never thought she would feel.

It was a sense of accomplishment that she would never forget. How could anyone forget their first lesbian experience? How could anyone forget when they finally came out and found the happiness that they'd wanted for such a long time? It was everything that she had wanted and imagined. But somehow, it was even better than that.

She leaned down and kissed Tia when she was finished coming. It was a long and sensual kiss. She wanted to let Tia know that she had zero regrets and that Tia was going to be a part of her future.

Who Is in Charge Tonight?
by John Sharma

"HERE, TASTE THIS." He held the spoon up to her mouth and waited until she inched closer, her red lips parting open. Her tongue darted out, and she licked the sauce off, her eyes widening in surprise.

"Mm, that's really good." Jill smiled, her hazel eyes lit up with amusement. "Are you sure you're not having some hot date over while I'm gone?"

"You're the only hot date I want," Perry replied, pausing to give her a quick peck on the lips. "Besides, you know that I'm trying new stuff out for my cooking class."

Jill stepped away from the stove and hopped onto the kitchen counter, letting her legs dangle over the edge. "So does this mean you're the one who's going to be doing all the cooking from now on?"

"It sounds like you want me to."

"As long as you're offering," Jill teased, pausing to place her bag on the counter next to her. "It would be a shame to let the lessons go to waste."

With a grin, he switched off the stove and spun around to face her. His wife sat in her knee-length black dress, a shawl draped over her shoulders, and her lips painted a bright red. She swung her legs back forth, her silver heels glistening underneath the florescent lighting of the kitchen.

She had never looked more beautiful.

He bridged the gap between them, placed one hand on either side of her on the counter, and kissed her. "Are you sure I can't convince you to stay in tonight?"

Jill sighed and linked her hands behind his neck. "I can't cancel on the girls again. Marissa said she would literally kill me."

He wrenched his lips away and pressed his mouth to her neck, inhaling the floral scent of her perfume. Then his hands moved to her waist, and he dug his nails into the soft flesh there, feeling her goosebumps through the thin fabric of her dress.

Perry knew she wanted him too.

Almost as much as he wanted her.

She angled her head, giving him better access,

and he kissed a path down to her cleavage, pausing to push her breasts together. Her breath hitched in her throat as she spread her legs open and locked them around his waist. Perry's pulse quickened as he rubbed himself against her, and she moaned.

"I can make it worth your while." Perry kissed a path up to her neck and nipped the sensitive flesh there. Her hands moved from his hair to his shoulders, and she squeezed, sending dual waves of pain and pleasure ricocheting through him.

After five years of marriage, Jill still knew exactly what to do in order to get under his skin, but tonight was different. For the past year, the two of them had been struggling to keep things interesting; they'd tried everything from watching porn together to entertaining the idea of a threesome.

Months later, Perry was beginning to wonder if this was the key all along.

"How will you make it worth my while?"

Perry drew back to look at her, and her lips parted in a whimper. "I get to make all the rules."

Jill's eyes widened. "What?"

"For one night, I get to make all the rules," Perry repeated with a smirk. "And we get to pretend we're not a boring old married couple."

Jill chuckled. "We're not a boring old married couple."

Perry lowered his head and kissed her soundly. "Prove it."

Jill's phone rang, piercing through the silence. She glanced down at her purse, and Perry growled, bringing his head to a rest in the crook of her neck. Reluctantly, Jill placed a hand on his chest and shook her head. Once she unlocked her legs from around his torso, he took a step back and exhaled.

She jumped off the counter, smoothed out the front of her dress, and reached for her purse. When she pressed the phone to her ear and drifted away, he stared at her back and the sway of her hips. Jill drifted closer to the front door, pushed the curtain aside, and peered out into the darkness. Perry cast a quick look over his shoulder at the oven before he crept forward and held his breath.

As soon as he came to a stop behind Jill, she stiffened. "It's okay. Of course I don't mind if you're a little late. I'll be waiting anyway."

Perry grinned and wrapped his arm around her waist. "Tell her she can be as late as she wants."

Jill giggled and tried to squirm away. "No, that's Perry. Don't worry about it."

He pushed her hair forward and pressed a kiss to

the back of her neck. A moment later, the hairs on the back of her neck rose, and Jill sagged against him, her round, firm ass pressed against his front. Perry's heart thudded against his chest as he shifted and rubbed himself against her back.

"Call me when you're outside," Jill whispered in a thick voice. "I'll see you soon, Mar. Bye."

With trembling fingers, Jill put her phone back in her purse and set it down on the table next to her. Meanwhile, Perry continued to press kisses to the back of her neck and nibble on her lobes. His hands moved up and down her bare arms, leaving a trail of heat in his wake. She shuddered and twisted an arm over her head, threading her fingers through his hair.

"We can't do this now," Jill murmured with a sigh. "We don't have time."

"We have plenty of time," Perry disagreed with a shake of his head. "All you have to do is let go and follow my head."

Jill spun around and captured her lips with his.

He cupped her face in his hands and deepened the kiss, pausing to run his tongue along her lower lip. She gasped, and as soon as her mouth parted, he slid his tongue in, beginning a sensual battle for dominance. Jill pressed her back against the wall, and he kicked her legs open.

As soon as she rubbed herself against him, all sane thought flew out the window. With a growl, he hoisted her up and carried her into the bedroom, never once breaking their kiss. In the doorway, he fumbled with the knob until Jill reached behind her and shoved it open. Heart thundering wildly in his ears, he stopped to set Jill down on the bed and take a step back.

"Perry—"

"I'm not Perry. Tonight, I'm…Ricardo."

Jill's eyes turned molten. "Ricardo, I don't have a lot of time."

"I can be quick," Perry promised her, stopping to kick off his shoes and pull his shirt up over his head. He pulled his pants down and smirked. "But not so quick that you won't enjoy it."

Jill's tongue darted out to lick her lips. "I can't wait."

All of the blood rushed to Perry's groin as his wife sat up and twisted her arms behind her head. He heard the zipper slide down and realized he was making a low growling sound in the back of his throat. Once the dress pooled around her waist, Jill stood up and let it fall into a heap on the floor. In a black bra and matching panties, she was the most beautiful thing he'd ever seen.

Especially bathed in the soft glow of the silver moon.

"Let me undress you," Perry said in a hoarse voice. Jill held still as he unhooked her bra and pulled her panties down over her knees before letting them fall to the floor. Once they did, he straightened his back and claimed her mouth with his.

The sound of her whimpers almost sent him over the edge.

"Let me take off my shoes," Jill murmured into the kiss. "Or do you want me to keep them on?"

"Keep them on," Perry replied, stopping to pinch her nipples. "You didn't tell me what your name was."

"My name is Celine," Jill replied breathlessly. "I'm really glad we ran into each other tonight."

"I knew from the moment I set eyes on you that we were going to end up here." Perry maneuvered them so they were falling backwards onto the mattress. He pinned her arms over her head and kissed a path over her chest, down to her pussy and paused. His gaze rose up to meet hers, and he saw a thin sheen of sweat break out over her forehead. With a grin, he kicked her legs open and settled in between them.

Perry ran his tongue over the smooth, tanned

skin, stopping when he reached her pussy. Then he began to place hot, open-mouthed kisses along the inside of her thighs, grunting when Jill's fingers wound themselves through his hair. He inserted one finger in between her wet folds and another.

Jill arched her back and moaned. "Oh, Ricardo. You know exactly how to please a woman, don't you?"

"I'm going to worship every inch of your body," Perry promised before flashing her another smile. "All I need you to do is surrender control, okay?"

Jill lowered her gaze and looked him directly in the eyes. "I'm all yours."

"You're all mine," Perry echoed, his tongue darting out to lick a path up to her nub. He removed both fingers and plunged his tongue in when she whimpered. Jill cried out, and her grip on the back of his head tightened, sending dual waves of pain and pleasure ricocheting through him.

He dug his nails into her waist and squeezed his eyes shut.

Her juices coated every inch of his mouth as he sucked and lapped, enjoying every minute of it. Her hands fell on either side of the mattress and gripped the sheets tightly. He forced one eye open and looked up at her. Perry lowered his head and ran his tongue back and forth.

When her breathing turned heavy and she began to buck against him, Perry's movements grew faster and more frantic. He dragged his tongue back and forth until she came undone, chanting his name as she did. As soon as her breathing returned to normal and her grip went slack, Perry glanced up at her and grinned. Both eyes flew open and pinned him with a pointed look.

"Aren't you going to fuck me?"

Perry made a low guttural sound in the back of his throat. "I'm going to fuck your brains out, Celine."

With that, he hoisted himself up and positioned himself at her entrance. In one quick move, he was inside, filling every inch of her. Jill raked her fingers over his back and lifted her hips up off the mattress. She met every thrust with one of her own until the bed began to creak and groan underneath them. Jill linked her legs over his torso and drew him closer.

Every part of him was on fire.

And she was the only solution.

The sound of her phone pierced through the silence, and he brought his head to a rest against the headboard. "Ignore it. Nothing else matters, Celine. We only have tonight. This is all we get."

Jill cried out and sank her nails into his back. "Oh, *Ricardo*. Oh, yes."

"You want me to keep fucking you, don't you? Nothing else matters, does it?"

"Nothing else matters," Jill repeated in a strangled voice. "Oh, God. *Oh, yes*. Yes, right there."

Perry braced his hands on either side of the headboard and thrust in and out of her, the sound of her heavy breathing filling his head. Using her fingers, she traced the entire length of his back, stopped at his ass, and squeezed. He reached for her hands, held them up over her head, and groaned.

Then he lowered his head and took one nipple between his teeth.

Jill bucked.

He moved to the other nipple, and her breathing quickened. "Don't stop, Ricardo. Don't ever stop."

"I won't." He gave a few more thrusts before he came inside her with a grunt and a moan. Jill's own release followed soon after, and she clung to him as she shook and writhed. Once he was able, he eased out of her and collapsed onto the bed next to her. A few moments later, Jill sat up and scrambled off the bed.

"Thanks, Ricardo, but I've got somewhere to be."

Perry rolled over onto his side and propped himself up using one elbow. "I feel used."

Jill leaned over and gave him a quick kiss. "Maybe I'll see you again."

Perry smiled. "I hope so."

In a flurry, Jill hurried around the room, picking up her clothes and muttering to herself. When he heard the shower running, Perry rose off the bed and padded toward her. In the doorway to their shared bathroom, Jill called out to him to answer her phone.

Perry exhaled, reached for his sweatpants, and hurried into the living room. He grabbed her purse off the counter and pressed the phone to his ear. "Jill spilled something on her clothes. She's taking a shower now."

"You and your cooking lessons," Marissa complained with a sigh. "All right. I'm parking outside. Mind if I come in and wait?"

"Go ahead."

When Jill came back out, in the same outfit, without a single hair out of place, it took everything he had not to reach for her again. He imagined taking her back into the bedroom for an entire night of fun, but she gave him a quick look that stopped him in his tracks. On her way out, she blew him a kiss and a wink over her shoulders.

Perry spent the rest of the night in the study on the treadmill, trying to work off the extra energy. Eventually, after a quick meal and a bottle of beer, he crawled into bed and stared at the ceiling. Before he drifted off, he heard Jill giggling and the clatter of shoes. He threw off the covers and came out as she slammed the door shut.

She gave him a messy kiss on her way to the bathroom.

Jill fell asleep seconds after her head hit the pillow. Perry curled himself around her and pressed a kiss to the back of her neck. Hours later, when bright sunlight poured in through the open curtains, Perry frowned and sat up. He rubbed a hand over his face and kicked the covers off. In a daze, he stumbled to the curtains and yanked them shut.

Once he spun around and saw Jill standing in the doorway, in a French maid's costume, his mouth fell open. "What's happening?"

"Did you forget that I was coming again, sir?" Jill held up the feather duster and stepped into the room. "It's okay. I can clean the room while you're in here."

Perry slammed his mouth shut. "Is there anything I can do to help?"

Jill giggled. "Why don't you sit down on the bed and press your wrists together?"

Perry did as he was told, the blood roaring in his ears. "Okay, what's next?"

Jill pulled a tie out of her back-pocket and bound his wrists together. "Now you have to do exactly what I say, or I'm going to punish you."

Perry's eyes moved over her and stopped when they reached her mouth. "What do you want me to do?"

"Francesca wants to have some fun." Jill tossed the feather duster over her head and climbed onto his lap. She rocked back and forth against him, her breasts straining against her outfit. "I want to make sure you're ready for me."

"I'm ready." Perry growled into her neck. "Look how hard you're making me."

Jill batted her lashes at him. "It has to be enough, Mr. Spence. I don't think it's enough."

"Why don't you take my pants off, and you'll see?"

Jill stood up and wagged a finger at him. "You're still going to be punished, Mr. Spence."

Perry nodded and said nothing.

Abruptly, she drew him to his feet and pulled down his pants. As soon as she did, his erection sprang free, and she made a low delighted noise. She pushed him back onto the bed and climbed on top of him, hoisting her outfit up so it was around her waist. When she lowered herself onto him, his eyes rolled to the back of his head, and he cursed.

"You were right, Mr. Spence. You are hard."

"Only for you."

"You have to fuck me hard, Mr. Spence," Jill whispered into his ear. "Like your life depends on it."

Perry groaned and thrust upwards until he reached the hilt. "How's this?"

Jill threw her head back and moaned. "Harder."

Together, they rocked back and forth with Jill leaving hot, open-mouthed kisses on his neck, his chest, and against his lips. Every time he moved to deepen the kiss, she wagged a finger at him and drew back. When her hands moved to her breasts and pushed them together, Perry thought he was going to explode.

Suddenly, she unbound his wrists and placed both hands on her hips. "I want you to undress me now."

Perry helped her out of her clothes, but she

stopped him with a quick look at the bed. "I want you to stand in front of the bed."

She waited until he did before she climbed onto the bed and gave him her back. Then she got down on all fours and threw him a look over her shoulders. "Fuck me, Mr. Spence. Fuck me hard and fuck me good."

In one quick move, Perry thrust inside of her.

He slammed in and out of her until she was crying out and chanting his name. "What do you want me to do now?"

"Slap my ass," Jill breathed. "Hard."

Perry's heart pounded against his ears. "God, you're so sexy."

Over and over, the two of them rocked back and forth until Jill came, her entire body shaking and writhing. Perry's own release followed soon after as he exploded inside of her and went limp. As soon as he was done, he eased out of her and collapsed onto the mattress. Jill tucked herself into his side and nuzzled against his neck.

"I like this dominant side of you," Perry said into her hair. "We should see more of her."

"I think so too," Jill agreed with a kiss. "I'm starving. We should get something to eat."

One, Two, Three
by Genevra Wilson

ALICE LOOKED at her watch for what felt like the hundredth time today.

When is this hell going to be over?

The professor's voice had been drowned out half an hour ago by the excitement that came with knowing that in two hours, she was going to be meeting Phil and Sawyer for lunch. Honestly, time couldn't move fast enough. She tapped her pen against her open copybook of empty pages and looked across the lecture hall for anything to distract her and calm her down.

College was a drag.

To be perfectly frank, she had no idea why she had agreed to this in the first place. Her parents weren't exactly struggling, and she knew she could have just gone to community college back in Arizona where their contacts would have made sure she didn't really have to do anything. But no, she had wanted to get out from under their shadow. She had wanted to explore the big, bad world and become her own little trailblazer.

She mentally slapped herself. She'd been doing that a lot lately.

The truth was, the world she wanted to explore was pretty much the same everywhere she went, or at least on this side of the Atlantic. Sure, there was the infatuation with discovering a new city, a new state for that matter, but that lasted what? A few weeks? Soon enough, she was bored and agitated. When she boiled it down to the basics, the people were the same, the places were the same, even the fucking coffee was the same.

Which was why her chance encounter with Phil and Sawyer Lloyd had been a much-needed change from the status quo.

"Miss Gordon." The professor's voice brought her back to the present. "Care to elaborate on this theory?"

"Not really," Alice replied. "It's all quite abstract anyway."

A few students chuckled, and the professor

frowned at her. "Abstract? Are you sure you're in the right class?"

He didn't wait for her to reply before moving on to torture someone else.

Alice looked at her watch again.

She had met the Lloyds a couple of months back during one of her shifts at the Coffee Bean. They had seemed like your typical corporate couple, him with a dark suit that screamed *I have a killer body underneath this*, and she with a skirt, blouse and heels that gave quite the view of legs any man would want wrapped around them. And they were definitely in love, touching each other's hands, laughing, talking as if they had been on a date and not a lunch break.

They had caught Alice staring once and had called her over, asking her all sorts of questions like where she was from, what she was studying, how long had she been in the city. Looking back, one could easily say the intrusiveness could have come off as creepy, but Alice had given up the information easily in return for a great conversation that got her a lot of heat from her manager later.

They kept coming to the Coffee Bean, and she kept getting to know them better. Not to mention the nights of erotic fantasy she'd had of both of them.

Bent over the barista station while Phil fucked her from behind. Having Sawyer go down on her and make her scream. Could anyone blame her? They were both hot as fuck, and for some reason, they were interested in her.

And she had a feeling they weren't totally ignorant of how attractive she was either.

Alice never considered herself a bombshell, but she knew she could pull off a killer bikini, and her ash-brown locks with her blue eyes often made heads turn. She smiled when she remembered running into the Lloyds at the beach. She could have been caught salivating. Phil, chiseled as promised, tanned to perfection, dark hair framing hazel eyes that seemed to bore into your soul. And Sawyer, looking like she had just walked out of a photo shoot, long legs and firm breasts immediate eye-catchers if you could ignore the pixie-cut blond hair that accented the most gorgeous emerald eyes.

To this day, Alice would get goosebumps remembering the way Sawyer had bitten her lower lip when taking her in. And Phil had definitely been making an effort to maintain eye contact.

"Okay, that's all for today," came the wonderful dismissal from the tyrant below.

Alice jumped from her seat, grabbed her books,

and quickly made her way out of the lecture hall before anyone could stop her. She raced out into the scorching heat and made her way quickly toward the parking lot. A few of her friends called out to her, and she waved hello and pointed at her watch. She didn't have time for chit-chat. Her entire body shook with the excitement of finally being able to spend some quality time with the Lloyds.

Her phone chimed, and she looked down at the text message from Sawyer. It was a location, and Alice frowned when she realized it wasn't where they had agreed to meet. Then the phone rang, Sawyer's gorgeous profile picture flashing.

"What happened? I thought we were having lunch," Alice asked.

"We've moved it to our place," Sawyer replied. "Phil has a call that might take a while, so we didn't want to keep you waiting. Besides, I've already started on the chicken parmesan. Hope you're hungry!"

The food was incredible.

Actually, everything about the day had been incredible. The gorgeous house, the incredible wine, the lovely conversation. It was far better than she had ever imagined. Of course, it didn't hurt that the Lloyds were a lot more laid back when on home turf. Sawyer's summer dress couldn't have been flimsier, and Phil in shorts and shirt were mwah, chef's kiss.

Sprawled on the couch next to Sawyer in a living room with a view of the ocean, wine in her hand, Alice felt like she was in heaven.

"How do you guys ever leave the house?" Alice asked.

Phil laughed, refilled the ladies' wine glasses, and sat down on the opposite loveseat. "Work forces us to."

"Seems incredibly unfair."

"It is," Sawyer giggled. "If you stand over by the fake fireplace, you actually get to see a large portion of the beach."

Alice stood up and walked to where Sawyer was pointing, taking in the view. From this angle, she had a pretty good view of the entire beachside row of the city, and it took her breath away. "It's beautiful."

Two slender arms wrapped around her from behind, and she closed her eyes as she breathed in Sawyer's perfume. "It really is," Sawyer said. Softly, she kissed the nape of Alice's neck. "Extremely beautiful."

Alice took another sip of her wine as Sawyer pushed the top straps off and kissed her shoulders. Something inside of her lit up, and heat raced through her. The kisses continued, and Sawyer's hands snaked around her waist, pushing the top up until her hands were gently caressing her bra. Alice somehow found the ability to place her glass on the mantle without dropping it and slowly turned around to face the blonde. Their lips connected immediately, and Sawyer's kiss almost sent Alice to her knees.

Sawyer led them back to the couch, lips exploring each other's necks, shoulders, and faces. Alice's top was quickly disposed of, and her flip-flops were forgotten somewhere along the way. Sawyer smiled at Phil, and he joined them at the couch, sitting down so that Alice's head rested on his lap while Sawyer pulled her shorts off.

Alice couldn't believe what was happening. She had always had fantasies about the Lloyds, but that was all she had ever expected them to be. Fantasies. Never in her wildest dreams had she imagined this would be happening.

Phil bent down and kissed her, the taste of wine on his lips and tongue intoxicating, the smell of his cologne making her head spin. Sawyer was unclasping the front of her bra, and when Alice broke away from Phil's kiss, she was greeted with the beautiful view of the blonde licking circles around her nipple.

"She's gorgeous, Phil," Sawyer whispered.

"She sure is," Phil replied and kissed Alice again.

Sawyer stood up and let her summer dress drop. Wearing nothing underneath, Alice looked upon the naked body of a goddess. She could feel the wetness between her legs soak through her panties just imagining what she would do to that body, and what Sawyer would do to her. The image of his wife obviously excited Phil, too, because his erection was hard against Alice's neck, and the size of him kind of scared her.

"You're a lot hotter than I imagined," Alice croaked.

Sawyer smiled. "You imagined?"

"How could I not?"

Sawyer giggled and hooked two fingers into Alice's panties, pulling them off slowly. Sawyer kissed her way from Alice's feet to the back of her knees, to the inside of her thighs until the woman had both legs open and was blowing softly against Alice's pussy.

Alice was already beginning to squirm.

Phil lowered her head to the couch, stood up, and undressed, watching his wife intently. Alice could have sworn he had just jumped out of a *GQ*, and when he came closer, she reached out and grabbed his cock, her fingers barely closing around it.

"I'd love to see you in her mouth," Sawyer said, and before Alice could reply that she shared the sentiment, Sawyer's tongue found her clit. Alice gasped, her hand shooting down to grab the other woman by the hair, then almost screamed when Sawyer's tongue began its assault on her pussy. Phil moved even closer, and Alice took him into her mouth, his cock forcing her to open wide, his grunt of satisfaction like music in her ears.

Sawyer used her tongue the way an artist would use their paintbrush, creating a masterpiece across the canvas that was Alice's pussy. Alice arched her back with every new shock of pleasure that shot through her, and Phil's cock in her mouth only added to the excitement she was feeling. She lost track of time, and before she knew it, she was shaking with an orgasm like she had never felt before, hands on Sawyer's head and legs shaking uncontrollably.

Phil pulled out of her mouth and gently pulled Alice to her feet, turning her around while Sawyer sat back and opened her legs. "My turn," Sawyer said with a wink.

Alice took in the musk of her, and she could already see that Sawyer was wet with desire. The older woman was massaging her breasts and let out a small moan as Alice kissed her thighs and slowly made her way to her pussy. Sawyer's fingers entangled themselves in Alice's hair as she guided her, and when Alice's mouth finally descended on the hot, wet core of the older woman, Sawyer moaned loudly in approval.

Phil crawled onto the couch and positioned himself behind Alice, lifting her hips up. The tip of his cock massaged her pussy lips, sliding up and down and driving her insane before finally pushing inside her. He was so big she almost screamed at the girth of him. He took it slowly, sliding in inch by inch, squeezing her ass until he was all the way inside.

"Sawyer, she feels so good!" he said.

Sawyer wasn't listening, though. Alice's tongue was lapping at her wetness, pushing into her pussy before flicking at her clit. Her grip on Alice's hair tightened as she rocked her hips, Alice's tongue and mouth ravishing her. Phil began to move, pulling out and then pushing back in, slowly at first and bit by bit picking up the pace. Soon he was fucking Alice with all he had, her ass slapping against his pelvis.

Alice was in heaven. Sucking on Sawyer's clit, Phil's cock in her own pussy, it was all more than she could fathom. She had dreamed of this, had masturbated constantly to it, but to actually be between the two of them was on a completely different level. She could never in her wildest dreams have imagined that the couple from the Coffee Bean would be the very same that was making her body shake with one orgasm after the other.

Phil pulled out of her and smacked her ass, then bent down and licked her pussy. Alice's screams of pleasure could have been deafening if not for Sawyer's pussy muffling her. Sawyer's humping against her face intensified, and soon enough, the woman was shaking with her own orgasm.

Alice felt strong hands pick her up until she was standing on the couch, looking down at a post-orgasm Sawyer, who was still shaking. She watched as Phil helped her to her feet, then lay down on the couch. He grabbed Alice's thighs and guided her down so she was sitting on his face, and shock waves shot through her as his tongue began working her core. Sawyer smiled and straddled her husband, gently pumping his cock and watching Alice in heat.

"He does that so well, doesn't he?" She smiled.

Alice could only nod. She could already feel her next orgasm coming on.

Sawyer lifted her hips and slid her husband's cock inside her, sighing in delight as she pushed him all the way in. Alice watched the other woman move, grinding against Phil, riding him hard. Her breasts bounced, and Alice moved in and took one in her mouth, sucking hard on the nipple and nibbling on it. Sawyer held her to her chest as she fucked her husband, and Phil's tongue was starting to do things to Alice that she had never felt before. Her orgasm hit without warning, and she clenched her thighs against Phil's head. His hands squeezed her ass, and he doubled down on his efforts, forcing her into a frenzy of multiple orgasms.

Sawyer's movements intensified, and soon she was riding her husband like her life depend on it. She grabbed Alice and dug her nails into her back, and when her orgasm hit, she shook so hard, both women almost fell off the couch.

"So good," Sawyer gasped. "So fucking good."

Alice crawled off Phil's face, her world spinning. She fought the urge to collapse on the couch and just call it a night, and when she felt Phil's hands on her hips, she knew he wasn't done with her just yet.

Sawyer sat back on the couch as Phil flipped Alice on her back. Her head nestled in Sawyer's lap, and the other woman started to gently play with her breasts and nipples.

"Not quite done here." Phil smirked.

Alice had no idea how much more she had in her, but Phil's stamina was turning her on, and this time, when he pushed his cock inside her, there was no resistance at all. She was so wet, he could have been double the size and it wouldn't have mattered.

"Fuck her, baby," Sawyer coaxed. "She likes it, don't you, Alice?"

"I do..." Alice moaned when Phil pulled out and pushed back in.

"See?" Sawyer giggled. "She's enjoying this just as much as we are."

Phil lifted both of Alice's legs up, pushing even deeper inside her, forcing her to squeal. He licked the soles of her feet, upping his pace as he fucked her, sucking on her toes, slamming into her hard. Alice was intoxicated with all the triggers she was feeing at the same time. Sawyer reached down and began playing with her clit, and when Phil increased his pace, Alice's screams were deafening.

One orgasm hit her after the other, but Phil wasn't slowing down. She could feel him pulsing inside her, and with every stroke, he hit parts of her she had never known could be hit. Sawyer kissed her, fondled her, and fingered her clit until Alice could take no more. Her final orgasm hit her like a hurricane, and she shook so hard, Sawyer had to hold her tight to stop her from falling off the couch.

"That's a good girl," Sawyer laughed. "Easy now, easy. Phil, you almost killed her."

Phil chuckled. Alice barely opened her eyes to see him stroking his cock, watching her nestled between his wife's breasts. He bent down and kissed her thighs, and Sawyer pushed him gently away with one foot.

"We don't want to break her, honey," she said. "I want to keep her for a while."

Alice tried to catch her breath, her heart thumping in her chest.

"Come here, I'll take care of that," Sawyer coaxed.

Alice looked up and watched Sawyer take her husband into her mouth. Effortlessly, she began sucking him, her head bobbing. Her tongue licked up and down the man's huge cock, swirling circles around his tip, then taking him in her mouth again. This continued for a while until Phil reached down and grabbed his wife by the hair, fucking her mouth as if he were fucking her pussy.

Alice was impressed by how Sawyer took it, no sign of any discomfort, obviously used to what her husband was doing. Phil suddenly pulled out, and before Alice could move, he exploded across Sawyer's breasts, some of his cum falling on Alice's cheek.

"Look at that, Phil, you made a mess on our friend," Sawyer giggled. She moved Alice's head and licked the cum off her face, then kissed her. "You did so well."

Alice smiled. Not only was she tired, but she had never felt this relaxed and satisfied in her life.

"Tell you what," Sawyer whispered. "How about I lend you a change of clothes, and you spend the night?" She looked up at Phil. "We do have room for Alice, don't we, honey?"

"All the room she needs," Phil said with a smile.

Alice closed her eyes and felt her entire body begin to soar.

"What do you say, Alice?" Sawyer asked.

And just before she fell into a deep sleep, Alice whispered, "I'd love to."

Big Enough for Sheri
by Celeste Watts

EVERYTHING HAD BEEN GOING great for Richard. But that wasn't going to last long. It never lasted long.

Because Richard had a small dick. It wasn't something that should have been as important to him as it was. But, the complex often ruled him. It wasn't the fact that he felt stunted. It was the fact that he felt like he could never please his Black wife Sherie, a woman who had predominantly only dated Black males before she landed on White Richard. The race didn't really matter. But he couldn't turn down the fact that all of her exes, who had been Black males, had bigger dicks than he did. That was the problem with an honest wife. She never thought to hide anything from him, nor did he want her to. He needed to know how big their dicks were. Because even if he didn't know that they had big dicks, he knew that he was little. He didn't need to compare it to anything else.

But outside of all that mental language that plagued him on a daily, everything was going well while he and his wife walked through the grocery store. This was where he felt happiest with her. He liked taking her out to dinner and taking her shopping even if it was for groceries because it felt like he was providing for her. Which he was. If he couldn't please her in the bedroom, he could at least please her financially. Of course, she didn't care about any of that. She loved him. She didn't even care about his dick size. But he cared about his dick size. He always felt like he was letting her down in the bedroom even when she would come. And that had gone on for ten years. Over that decade, he had learned how to keep it at bay. But it wasn't the easiest thing to pull off. When it came to its dick, it was more like a monster he kept hitting away. The monster was his insecurity.

"I want to get smoked salmon today. Where would they have that?" he asked his wife as they walked through the aisles.

"Probably in the seafood department. Let's go over and check."

As they rounded the aisle, down by the seafood was a man named Anthony. Richard's heart sank.

He only knew the man's name because of how much he had creeped him out on Facebook. He also creeped him out on Instagram. And this was because Anthony was Sheri's last boyfriend. Of course, the one thing that Richard fixated on with the man had been his penis. The man nearly had an eight-incher. Richard's three couldn't compete. It haunted him. It shouldn't have haunted him after ten years, but it still did, especially given the fact that he was right before them both.

"Oh my God. We can turn around," his wife said.

"No. He already saw us. It's okay." He continued to walk toward Anthony even though his wife was hesitant.

Anthony even looked taken aback. They'd had conversations in the past. But that was years ago, maybe even seven.

"Hey man, how are you?" Richard asked. His heart was racing. He hated that it was. He hated that he still had a complex. All he wanted to do was get over his insecurities. He couldn't help but realize that confronting Anthony was one way of doing that.

"Hey, guys! How have guys been? I'm good. You look great, Sheri."

Richard looked over to his wife to see how she would react to that comment. He couldn't tell whether or not she got flustered by it. Her voice did change, though. When she spoke, it was a little high-pitched. A little cutie. "Thank you. You don't look too bad yourself. It's been a very long time."

"Yes, ma'am," Anthony said. "Time really flies."

"Have you gotten married?" Richard asked. He kind of felt silly asking that because he knew the answer. The man never posted about women on Facebook. He was simply a player. And a man who was hung like that, who could blame him?

"Nope, I'm still single. I don't have luck with women. Just ask Sheri. Not to be disrespectful. I'm joking."

Richard made sure to laugh. Even though he knew the man wasn't joking. He had given his wife some of the best sex she ever had. She didn't tell Richard that. But he could tell. There has been a twinkle in her eye whenever she spoke about Anthony. He was a legend in her eyes. A sex legend. There was nothing that Richard could do to compete with him. At least when it came to his dick. There was only so much one could do with a tongue and fingers.

"Well, it was good seeing you, man. Come on,

Sheri, let's go home. Let's go pay for our stuff."

"What about your—"

"I'd rather really just pay for the stuff."

They walked to the line, and Richard knew that he hadn't handled that situation properly. He was embarrassed. After ten years, he still didn't have it under control. His complex still got the best of him.

"Richard, how could you act like that? You're the one that walked up to him. If you can't take the heat, then don't go into the kitchen."

"All right, whatever. I don't know what you want me to say."

His wife stayed quiet. He knew he'd messed up. There was no way around it. He had messed up royally. He'd let his emotions get the best of him.

Later that night, Sheri went to bed, but Richard couldn't sleep. The sight of Anthony was plastered all across his mind. He was downright restless.

Because of this, he wound up messaging him. His wife would have considered him crazy. Heck, most people would have considered him crazy. But he did it anyway.

"I want you to fuck my wife."

He had messaged Anthony on Facebook.

It wasn't long before Anthony messaged him with his phone number. "Let's talk."

**"

The following day was a Saturday. When Richard came down to his wife making breakfast, she seemed a little less angry at him, but there was still something there. There was a tension that he couldn't avoid. And rightfully so. It was probably going to get worse after he revealed what he'd spoken to Anthony about. The fact that he had gone behind her back was probably not the best thing. But it had happened, and there was nothing that she could do about it.

"Anthony is going to have sex with you. I know you want it. And it's been plaguing me for years. I want to face it. I want to watch it happen so that I can finally get over this," Richard said to her without even a good morning.

She put her spatula to the side and turned off the flame to what had to be eggs. When she turned around, she folded her arms and looked Richard in the eyes. "Fine. If this is what you want, then I'm not going to fight it. And you're going to have to just watch him fuck me."

Richard stayed quiet for a moment because there was a little bit of shock in his system. He had expected an argument. He had expected her to be pissed off. "That's it? You're not going to put up a fight or anything?"

She let out a sigh and looked at the floor. "What's the point in putting up a fight? Really think about that question. If I really turned it down and didn't have sex with Anthony, you would always think about it. It would plague you for the rest of your life. So if this is how you want to face it? Then so be it. And we'll see if we survive after you watch him run his cock inside of me."

Adrenaline and fear ran through him. On one hand, he wanted to do it, and on the other, he was unsure of how he would feel about it. But if one thing was for certain: It was happening. There were no ifs and or buts about it.

"All right, Sheri. Then let's schedule a date and have this happen."

Even though they scheduled their dirty meeting for two weeks later, those weeks had flown by. When it was time, Richard sat on the couch while Sheri sat on the other couch biting her nails.

"You don't have to do this if you're super nervous or something," Richard said. "Even though I don't know why you would be nervous. You already had sex with him years ago."

"Because I don't want this to affect our relationship. That's what I'm nervous about. I don't want anything to change."

"Nothing's going to change, baby. This is for me. This is for me to get myself right."

Her expression didn't change to amusement one or anything like that. Instead, she just looked anxiously frustrated. Richard could understand why. He definitely wasn't the easiest person to deal with. The situation that he had put her in was unprecedented. Especially after ten years together.

Taking him from his pity party, the doorbell rang. Both of their heads shot up in the direction of that door, knowing who was on the other side. They knew what that doorbell implied. It wasn't just any guest. It was going to be the guest that was going to have sex with her.

Richard was the one who made sure he answered the door. He didn't know why. But it felt right to do that.

When he opened it, there was Anthony and his over-six-foot self. He didn't look anything like they did. He was relaxed. His hands were in his pockets. He looked like he was just showing up at the DMV.

"Hey, Richard. How are you doing today?"

"I'm doing good. Come on in."

Richard decided that it was best he wasn't confrontational. Not that he was planning on doing that. But there could always be subtle ways where he didn't realize that he was coming off too strong.

When Anthony and Sheri looked they wanted another, you could feel the spark in the room. It was probably like turning on an old car and feeling that engine roar.

"How are you doing, Sheri? Are you ready for this?" Anthony asked.

"Yeah. Surprisingly I am. I psyched myself up last night."

Anthony laughed while Richard just observed. "You had to psych yourself up to have sex with me? I guess things do change, huh? She used to get so wet so quickly," he said to Richard.

It made Richard feel better that she would get wet really quickly with him as well. So that was something they had in common.

"Well, I'm married now. I really only have eyes for Richard but, you know. I guess I can dig deep to see if I'm still attracted to you somehow."

Anthony laughed yet again, and they all made their way up to the bedroom.

When they got there, it was a level of tension that Richard had never experienced. Just the three of them created this realm of uncertainty. Anthony was the one who broke it. The situation was about to unfold because he walked up to her and took her top off. It looked like he had been waiting to do that for a very long time. Perhaps he had been thinking about her more than Richard had realized.

It was such a sickening and relieving feeling to see his wife's clothes being taken off by another man. His worst fears were coming true. He could finally face them head-on. And that felt good. Watching it might have not felt good, but facing it did.

He wasted no time in taking her bra off. The way that he sucked her nipple, it almost looked like he was going to suck it right off. It had all begun. He was witnessing another man playing with his wife.

The biggest thing to realize for him was that she was enjoying it. It was the strangest thing to see, yet he had imagined it a million times. Somehow it wasn't as bad as he thought it would be. It was like exposure therapy. Once he saw it, he realized that it wasn't that bad at all.

His heart raced in anticipation of seeing Anthony rip her pants off. That came next. They came down, and her bush was in the room. He pushed her toward the bed and spread her legs wide open. Again he wasted no time and put his tongue between them. He licked like he was starving. He licked like he had been waiting ten years to re-lick her.

That was about as bad as it could get for Richard. The only thing left was to see that big dick of his enter into her. That was going to be the real test of how he was going to deal with the whole situation. Could he move on? Or would he always be stuck with his complex?

He would have to wait a bit to find that out because Anthony was taking his time eating her out. He was having a grand old time. Richard understood why. She had a great pussy. It always tasted fresh, and it was always wet.

When he was done feasting, he finally got up, took off his top, unzipped his pants, and what sprung out was not what he expected. It was a big dick. It was bigger than Richard's. But not by much. And that made Richard feel a little better. The second that he started to thrust into Sheri, his complex went away. There was a sense of accomplishment, like he had walked on the edge of a mountain, looked over the side, and slapped fear right in the face. That's what he did. He leaned back in his chair and watched his wife get fucked. He never had anything to fear after that. He'd watched the unthinkable. He'd done something that no other man could do. Or at least, not a majority of men. He was proud of himself.

What really touched him was the fact that Sheri had looked at him while she got railed. It was like she wanted Richard. Sure, there was some pleasure on her face. But for the most part, it looked like she just wanted Richard to be inside of her. He was most shocked by that. She really did love him. It was crazy to him to think that they had been together for ten years, and it had taken that little moment, that little bit of subtlety, to prove to him that she did love him unconditionally. Whether he had a small dick or a complex, it didn't matter to her. She loved him. And nothing was going to change that.

So was his complex completely gone? At that moment, that's exactly what it felt like. He looked forward to living the rest of his life with her. Because he knew that he had a woman who was devoted strictly to him. Complex or not, she loved him, and there was no bigger dick out there that could take her away from him. That was all he needed to see, and that was all he needed to know.

Because he loved Sheri with all his heart.

Conclusion

Thanks so much for taking the time to enjoy Orgasmic Erotic. I hope you had fun!

If you enjoyed it, please take a moment and leave a review! It'll only take a few seconds, and reviews really help new people find the book.

I'm already working on a follow-up, so please check back soon.

Until then, I hope all of your sexy fantasies come true.

Your new best friend,
Jade